John Paxton Sheriff was born in Liverpool and now lives in Wales.

THE CLUTCHES OF DEATH

When photographer Frank Danson took his wife Jenny to the theatre, they had two beautiful baby boys at home. But when they returned the boys had gone — presumably kidnapped. The loss was too great for Jenny to bear and Frank was left alone to grieve for his family. Then, twenty years later, the memories come screaming back. Who is sending him photographs hinting at unimaginable horrors, and taunting notes in blood? As the killings begin, amateur private eye Jack Scott must solve a mystery once buried in the past but now disinterred to make Frank's life a waking nightmare.

Books by John Paxton Sheriff
Published by The House of Ulverscroft:

A CONFUSION OF MURDERS

JOHN PAXTON SHERIFF

THE CLUTCHES OF DEATH

Complete and Unabridged

ULVERSCROFT
Leicester

First published in Great Britain in 2006 by
Robert Hale Limited
London

First Large Print Edition
published 2007
by arrangement with
Robert Hale Limited
London

British Library CIP Data

Sheriff, John Paxton
   The clutches of death.—Large print ed.—
Ulverscroft large print series: crime
1. Scott, Jack (Fictitious character)—Fiction
2. Missing children—Fiction 3. Private investigators
—Fiction 4. Detective and mystery stories
5. Large type books
I. Title
823.9′2 [F]

ISBN 978–1–84617–863–4

Published by
F. A. Thorpe (Publishing)
Anstey, Leicestershire

Set by Words & Graphics Ltd.
Anstey, Leicestershire
Printed and bound in Great Britain by
T. J. International Ltd., Padstow, Cornwall

For my wife, Patricia Ann

1

Day One — Monday 10 October

Midday, and I was in my workshop casting Ned Kelly bushranger sets for a military modelling shop in Cairns, Australia, when the man who had telephoned me from Liverpool about his murdered wife arrived at Bryn Aur.

The bullet that had raked my arm like rusty barbed wire aboard the moonlit yacht in Conwy harbour was, a week later, still giving me trouble. At odd moments during the night I would awake bathed in cold sweat as, in my dreams, I was once again holding in my blood-soaked arms the dying weight of Samantha Bone.

But that case was in the past. Work as well as time is the great healer, and I was bent over my centrifugal casting machine with an iron ladle in my gloved hands and the stink of hot tin alloy and rubber in my nostrils when Danny Maguire's Skoda popped gravel as he came rocking over the stone bridge.

I poked my head out into the sunshine where October wasps droned and the dry undergrowth tumbling down to the river

1

crackled in the heat of an Indian summer. Sultry. A suggestion of thunder in the air. My visitor was out of his car in the yard under the massive oak tree, tall and straight and turning slowly with his neck craned as he gazed up through the leaves to the soaring slopes of the Glyders where mountain sheep grazed without concern and the rocky peaks seemed to swing dizzily beneath thin, drifting clouds.

'Mr Maguire!'

He snapped his gaze down.

'I'll finish off here, and be with you.' I gestured. 'Go on into the house, pour yourself a drink of something.'

He lifted a hand, I caught the flash of white teeth, and he was gone. I went back into the workshop, removed the heavy black mould from the machine, clicked switches here and there and watched red lights blink out. Then I tossed my leather gloves on the bench alongside the ranks of glittering metal soldiers and walked up the slope with anticipation to meet my latest client.

He was standing in the hall, a crystal glass primed with amber liquid in one hand as he looked up the stairs at old stone walls where painted soldiers kept eternal, patient vigil in shaded niches. I kicked off my shoes in the porch, went through in my stockinged feet, grasped his wiry wrist as I leaned forward to sniff his glass. Islay, single malt. He'd chosen either the nearest decanter, the strongest drink, or he was a man who knew his whisky. But that was me conjuring up spirits to boost my ego, because the nearest decanter was the only decanter, and in the time available to him his choice had been limited to my expensive single malt or a tumbler of cold Welsh water from the tap.

'Half full, or half empty?' I released his wrist, let him work that out in the context of his own problem, nodded towards the big living-room and led the way inside. My socks whispered as I padded across the slate floor. Coolness touched my skin and I could smell the basket of birch logs by the inglenook, the still dust filming the bookshelves. He followed me through into the sunlit kitchen, from there into the office. The desk was unclut-tered. I sat in my swivel chair, flicked a hand towards the comfortable black leather arm-chair that was bursting at the seams. He settled himself gingerly and clutched his glass in both hands like a nervous fireman on a slippery pole.

I said, 'It's Danny, isn't it?' He nodded. 'Well, your phone message was blunt, Danny, and now you're here I assume your wife's not turned up?'

He shook his head.

'And you still believe she's dead?'

'Murdered?' He nodded. 'I know it.'

'No,' I said. 'You don't.'

He frowned. 'She's been gone for more than a week. There one day, gone the next — just like that.' He snapped his fingers.

'Your charm's faded, she's left you for another.'

'She's dead.'

'Dead is dead. Murdered is murdered. Which is it?'

'She . . . ' He hesitated. 'The people she meets in her work make the latter more likely.'

'But not inevitable.' I watched his eyes become unfocused as he sipped his drink. He'd asked to see me, but seemed loath to spill the beans. Maybe he was a politician. Maybe he was an ex-con. Maybe I was a private eye whose interviewing technique needed a polish.

He sighed, sank deeper into the chair.

'She makes prison visits. Meets violent, dangerous people. Befriends them.'

'Or makes enemies?'

He shrugged.

'And those prisoners are eventually released. Does she continue to see them on the outside?'

He nodded.

'How long's she been doing this?'

'Four or five years.'

I shook my head ruefully. 'That adds up to a lot of men out there who either love or hate your wife.'

'Or women.'

'What is it, a feminist group?'

'Not at all. A few years ago a small religious mission opened up in Woolton. Its lofty aims are to help prisoners all over the world. She became interested, then actively involved.'

He sipped his drink. Dark and thin, he seemed to flow with the leather chair's contours like a crumpled throw. But he'd phoned me with deep concern in his voice then left it for a full seven days before calling to see me. That seemed strange, and I put it to him.

'There's always hope, isn't there?' he said. 'And Calvin convinced me she'd turn up.'

'Calvin?'

'Calvin Gay. He runs the mission.'

'American?'

'I think so.'

'But he was wrong, and now you're here.' I watched him take another sip of the Islay. 'Why now? Why me? Why not the police?'

'You're Jack Scott, an amateur private eye with results a pro would envy. In the space of a couple of months, you and Calum Wick cleared up several murders. Here and in Liverpool.' For the first time he smiled, and I got a glimpse of the man behind the guarded blue eyes. 'What interests me is the way you located Gerry Gault, when he'd been missing a full year.'

'I found him, yes — but he'd been a long time dead.'

He didn't blink at the implication. 'However this turns out,' he said, 'I need to know.'

'You say your wife was there one minute, gone the next. Can you be more precise?'

'She set off early one morning to attend a conference of some kind. Out this way, Betws-y-Coed, the Waterloo Hotel, I think — you see, *your* home territory, that's another good reason for calling you.' He waited for a comment I didn't make, and said, 'She used her Suzuki 4 × 4. Took a colleague, Bill Fox.'

'For how long? A day, couple of days?'

'Just the one day. Afterwards — when she didn't come home — I phoned the hotel. They arrived, must have spent most of the day yacking in the conference suite, then left — and that's it.'

Yacking. That didn't sound like approval. I said, 'What about Fox?'

'I phoned Calvin to check. He got back OK.'

'Then surely Fox would have an idea where your wife is?'

'Maybe. Probably. But according to Calvin, he'd booked a holiday and is now soaking up the sun on a Greek island.'

'So he'll need someone with soft hands to rub Ambre Solaire on his back,' I said, and he looked at me with contempt.

He was making me twitchy. As limp as an empty sack, he was speaking when spoken to and volunteering nothing. 'I need to know,' he'd said, which sounded a lot less than urgent. I was sensing something beneath the surface, suggesting that the answer he got wouldn't concern him even if the news was bad. And aren't husbands always the first suspects when a wife dies violently?

I spun out of the chair with a mumbled excuse and left him to simmer gently in the silence and sort fact from fiction while I went through to the living-room and took a glass from the buffet. But the drink I was looking forward to wasn't to be. I had the decanter tilted in my hand and already clinking against the glass when the phone rang. It was DI Alun Morgan.

'If you're interested,' he said, 'there's a body been found in woods below Llyn Elsi.'

He'd named a lake in the wooded hills above Betws-y-Coed. Not a million miles

7

from the Waterloo Hotel. My hair prickled.

'Male or female?'

'Corpse is all I know,' he said. 'But you being on a roll, flavour of the month with your cap all bristling with feathers — '

'I'll meet you there.'

We were old friends, and he was doing me the kind of favour not usually associated with the police. I poured the drink, raised my glass to him and knocked it back. When I returned to the office Maguire detected something in my manner. In a flash his lean body went from limp to rigid, his eyes rimmed with white. And I couldn't help wondering if I was looking at a distraught husband fearing the worst, or a murderer realizing his victim had been found.

2

We drove to Betws-y-Coed in our own cars, left his Skoda and my Audi Quatro in Anna Davies's sloping car-park behind the Cotswold shop and walked up the road to the stony track that wound up through the woods to the lake.

The way into the trees was usually barred to motor vehicles, but the beam had been lifted for the police and their Range Rovers would have climbed with a roar of blue exhaust, stones flying from beneath cleated tyres. I crunched upwards without too much effort. Danny Maguire found the going tough. After a hundred yards he was panting and stumbling, slipping and sliding, his eyes drifting nervously to the crumbling verge and the steep drop on the left where white water tumbled and the rocks were slick and black.

When the curving path emerged from the trees and levelled off we took a breather, faces shiny with sweat, hands hooked on hips as chests heaved. Distant thunder rumbled. The skies above the valley were turning that ominous, lowering ochre. We set off again, took a right fork back into the trees and from there I sensed it would be just a short walk up the track because, in some strange way, I knew exactly where we would find the body.

We heard voices as we reached the next wide curve.

A single police Land Rover was parked half on the grass, its engine quietly ticking. The verge on the right fell away sharply for a few feet, then levelled. It was a lumpy, thickly wooded area of tough grass tussocks and pools of standing water alongside a sluggish stream where sunlight rarely filtered through the canopy of leaves. Today an errant shaft of light picked out the trunks of fallen trees, ragged ferns sprouting from the boggy earth.

Off the road in the midst of cold mountain water the air was dank. In front of us as we squelched between pools an ancient dry-stone wall snaked up the slope through trees and undergrowth, here and there just a tumble of fallen rocks, every inch of it green with moss. Maguire shivered; a sudden lightning flash was like an unseen cameraman recording his obvious apprehension.

The crime scene was marked off with tape.

DI Alun Morgan was standing with his hands thrust into the pockets of his jacket. He and a uniformed constable were looking down at a sprawled body. It was lying face up, as slack as a worn out bolster. The hair and much of the torso and limbs were half buried in damp leaves and broken twigs. Sunlight was reflecting off the mossy wall, turning the corpse's face and white shirt a pale green. In the centre of that chartreuse shirt there was a dark stain of dried blood.

Maguire made a soft, sick noise in his throat.

'Take it easy,' I said, my eyes on the corpse's flat chest. 'I don't know what your wife's like, but — '

'It's not her.' There was something in his voice. It didn't sound like relief.

Morgan had turned; he'd caught Maguire's words.

'Absolutely right,' he said, 'because it's a him not a her.' He turned his shrewd grey eyes on me, nodded at my companion. 'Who's this?'

'Danny Maguire, from Liverpool. His wife's missing.'

'And he can speak for himself,' Maguire said. His voice was tight. His eyes were fixed on the dead man. As we all followed his gaze the shaft of sunlight faded and died. Heavy drops of rain began pattering on the overhead leaves, reaching us as a fine spray that was cool to the skin.

'I know that man,' Maguire said.

I flashed him a glance. 'Don't tell me,' I

said with disbelief.

He nodded. 'Oh yes. That's Bill Fox.'

'Well, what he's soaking up here,' I said, 'has nothing to do with Greek islands or the hot sun.'

When Maguire looked up his eyes were haunted.

★ ★ ★

They took Danny Maguire to one side for a chat and through the mist of fine rain I looked idly about a crime scene that was going to provide forensics with a massive headache. The torn-up vegetation suggested a bit of a scuffle before violent death, but uniformed constables crawling around that boggy site were unlikely to come up with much more than wet knees, stained uniforms and black moods.

Maguire was mumbling answers, but from Alun Morgan's expression I knew that, so far, the police couldn't come up with the right questions.

After a while they gave up. Maguire had identified the body, nothing more, so Morgan asked me to keep him entertained while they looked for clues then wandered away with his black shoes squelching and his dark hair glistening in the rain. We were taken back down the hill in the police Range Rover, the wipers sweeping rain and wet leaves off the windscreen as we bounced and slid on stones that rolled beneath the tyres and set the vehicle yawing like a sloop in heavy weather.

Behind the Royal Oak the tables outside the Stables Bar appeared to be blanketed in mist as hard rain bounced off the stained boards. We ran inside. I ordered ice-cold Holsten for me, a double Scotch for Maguire, and from seats near the window we gazed out through the rain hammering on the road towards the deserted gift shops on the far side of the waterlogged park.

'Finding Fox doesn't help your search for your wife,' I said after a while, 'but, unfortunately, it does suggest another possibility.'

Suddenly an emotion I thought might be despair was dragging his face out of shape, deepening the lines. 'Possibility, or likelihood?' He looked at me. 'You mean my wife could be lying out there in those woods, don't you?'

'I don't know the full story — '

'You know as much as I do.'

'Do I?'

His head was lowered. He was toying with his drink, using the base of the glass to make shaky wet rings on the table.

I said, 'Danny, what was the connection between your wife and Bill Fox?'

He shook his head, lips pursed.

'What's her name?'

'Pat.'

'So, was I right? Pat has left you for another?'

'No.'

'But there's something you're not telling me.'

'I told you there was some risk in her work. Unsavoury characters. Well, there may be no connection, but she got a letter the day before she went missing.' He was blurting the words. His hand shook and the glass went bump on the table. 'Not exactly a letter.' He gestured vaguely. 'An index card. In an envelope. She'd ripped it open; I found it on her desk. There was writing . . . '

He was staring intently at nothing.

'Take your time.'

He shook his head. 'I'm all right. I was going to ask my wife what it meant, and then . . . '

I waited, deliberately gazed out of the window to take some pressure off him. The rain had died away. Alun Morgan's old Volvo estate came smoking along the road and turned into the Cotswold car-park. The Bethesda DI climbed out, glanced around, saw my face at the window and splashed across the forecourt and through the tables.

As he came in and glanced in our direction, Maguire gathered his thoughts and found his voice.

'It was unusual writing,' he said. 'Someone had used a thick red marker pen. On the white card. Block letters. It said, *Remember to forget.*'

'Whatever that might mean,' Alun Morgan said, steaming like a lean wet dog as he dropped into the empty seat. 'It's double Dutch as it stands — but she's your wife, after all, so I'm sure you'll be good at translating.'

★   ★   ★

The discovery of Bill Fox's body meant that Welsh detective Alun Morgan was conducting an investigation in which I had no place. Maguire had given me his telephone number and address, though both of us knew I'd been sidelined. With my mind elsewhere I knocked back my drink, left him to questioning by Alun Morgan that I was convinced would get neither of them very far, and made my way home to Bryn Aur.

The slate and gravel yard had been washed clean by the rain when I drove in and was gently steaming as it dried. I walked through knee-high mist and into the house, picked up the glasses we had abandoned when Alun Morgan phoned, rinsed them at the sink and looked out of the kitchen window towards the stone workshop while debating whether to go back to my casting.

A lot depended on Calum Wick. My Scottish colleague was currently painting sets of 15th Light Dragoons I'd based on figures illustrated in *The Thin Red Line*, a reference book by Donald and Bryan Fosten. They were shown unmounted, and the sets I'd designed consisted of four figures in various casual poses. The fine detail in uniforms and equipment would see Wick bent patiently over his work table with a tiny metal figure glistening in the light of the Anglepoise as he painted silver lace and buttons with a double-O Kolynsky sable. A single soldier would take as long to complete as a full set of Aussie bushrangers. Delivering more raw castings before he was ready would be a waste of time.

I went into the office and picked up the phone.

'There's coincidence,' Wick said when he answered.

'That's Welsh colloquial, and you're a Scot,' I said. 'And why is it coincidence?'

'Because I was about to call you. Knowing you'd be fascinated by a conversation I had at the Owl.'

'Go on.' He meant Night Owl, the Canning Street night club that had figured large in the Sam Bone case.

'With Frank Danson,' he said.

I waited.

'That name not ring a bell?'

'No.'

'Aye, well, taking into account your age and predilection for playing with wee toy soldiers — '

'Says he from his Grassendale flat where massed regiments of tiny figures are billeted. Get on with it, Cal.'

He chuckled. Something jingled wetly. I pictured him peering through smeared John Lennon glasses as he rinsed a paintbrush in white spirit.

'Twenty years ago,' he said, 'two boys disappeared from a house out Childwall way. Snatched. And that was it. Nothing more was heard. Ever.'

'Until now.'

'Aye. You'd better get in and talk to Danson, Jack. After all this time, someone's sending him photographs that'll make your bloody hair curl.'

3

I'd first encountered Calum Wick many years ago outside a rain swept spit-and-sawdust pub in Brixton. He had a fierce grin on his face, beneath the streetlights his black eyes glittered, and he was about to be beaten to a pulp by three huge Yardies. I was thirty-five, suntanned, fresh off the plane after five years in Australia. He was — well, he was Calum Wick, and in time I realized that was all I would ever know.

That night, shoulder to shoulder, we prevailed. The Yardies were vanquished, we retired from the scene to wash the blood of battle off faces and split knuckles in the ice-cold water of a cracked basin in an evil-smelling underground gents' toilet, and went on to become partners in a scam that involved ferrying expensive cars of dubious provenance over from Germany and selling them on through a bent Liverpool detective sergeant who had well-heeled contacts.

Neither of those activities could be called careers. Neither armed us with the skills needed to investigate violent crime. But before Australia and Calum Wick I had been a regular soldier, and over some fifteen years my tours with the Royal Engineers and SAS were complemented by a lengthy spell with the SIB — the army's Special Investigation Branch. When, disillusioned and conscience-smitten, I left Calum and his luxury car scam and began hitting the bottle, I was rescued and taken on by Manny Yates in his Lime Street firm of private investigators — a five year apprenticeship in investigation techniques that brings me in a roundabout manner to my interest in Calum Wick's news.

Roundabout because, in the time between Manny Yates and the gradual reawakening of my interest in the investigation of crime, I had discovered a talent for military modelling, bought the lonely Welsh farmhouse known as Bryn Aur that had become home and workshop, and set up business: Magna Carta — Military Miniatures for the Connoisseur. With Wick as a distant but irreplaceable colleague because the man I had first met splitting his knuckles on the skulls of those massive Yardies had found in hands too delicate for such violent work a skill with fine paint brushes to which Magna Carta owed much of its success.

He painted toy soldiers. He was an amateur private dick's assistant — rearrange those words as you will. And he continued flirting with scams I preferred not to look into too deeply.

Somewhere along the way, Sian Laidlaw arrived on the scene.

I was still smiling at warm memories of blonde-haired Sian, my ambitious Soldier Blue, when I crossed the Mersey at Runcorn, threaded the Quatro through the outskirts of Liverpool and began hunting for the home of a man who had lost his two boys, but never lost hope.

★ ★ ★

Frank Danson lived in an old but now fabulously expensive detached house in a close off Childwall Priory Road. Gravel crunched as I nosed the Quatro up to the double garage, then shifted beneath my feet as I climbed out of the car and made my way towards the steps leading to the front door. The gravel, I would learn, was as old as the mystery, but what struck me first when Frank Danson answered my ring at the doorbell was that here was a man who was probably several years younger than my creaking forty-eight, but who had hair that was almost snow white.

I'd phoned ahead, so he was expecting me. We shook hands. He led me inside. In a living-room that was as masculine as a

Foreign Legion barracks he offered me a drink, I accepted Becks straight from the fridge — no glass — and cuddling our bottles we sat bathed in evening sunlight slanting through windows that overlooked a back garden as long as a couple of cricket pitches.

After a while, with the level of beer considerably lower, he said, 'I don't know what to do.'

'Talk me through it.'

'How much did Calum Wick tell you?'

'You lost two boys twenty years ago. Heard nothing. Now someone's sending you photographs.' I winced. 'That sounds as bare and as cold as — '

'As the grave?'

'Damn,' I said. 'I'm making a mess of this.'

He smiled. 'No. I'm baiting you. Putting pitfalls in your way.'

'Then let me stick my neck out. You thought they were dead. After twenty years, what else could you think? But now that's changed.'

'Yes.' He sighed, looked at the beer bottle. 'Maybe. I don't know what to think.'

'Tell me what happened,' I said. 'Then — and now.'

He took a deep breath. 'Their names were Peter and Michael,' he said, and frowned at the past tense. 'Aged two and three. Jenny

21

and I were going to a show at the Playhouse. Usually her sister would baby-sit, but she was at a police conference in Scotland. A ~~young~~ girl was recommended; Tricia something or other. She arrived, we left to drive down town. When we got to the theatre, Jenny changed her mind. She was worried about the boys.' He looked up, smiled wryly. 'Usually that works out for the best, doesn't it? A change of mind averts your personal tragedy — you know, you decide not to go on a particular plane, it crashes and kills everyone on board.'

He shook his head. 'But it didn't work out like that. We arrived home — God, we'd been gone less than an hour — and the place was empty. No baby-sitter. No boys. No sign of life.' He swallowed. His wedding ring clinked against the bottle. 'And that was that,' he said huskily. 'I suppose the police did their best, but they got nowhere. We never saw the boys again.'

'And now?' I said softly.

He leaned forward, placed his empty bottle on the coffee table. A square of what looked like white card was lying alongside a silver box. Next to it was a colour transparency in a matt black mount. I'd done some photography. The transparency was the square, 6 × 6 format, probably taken using a camera like a

Hasselblad or a Bronica.

Danson picked up the white card, turned it over and handed it to me.

It was a 5″ × 5″ colour photograph of two men wearing black trousers and long-sleeved black sweaters, balaclavas pulled over their heads and faces. Their eyes glittered through sinister slits. They were standing against a wall, under an oil painting. I glanced across the room, saw the same painting, felt the hairs on my neck prickle.

'When did this arrive?'

'Twenty years ago.' He shook his head. 'I'm a professional photographer. When we got home that night the curtains were closed, but behind them I saw a flare of bright light and thought it was probably an electronic flash. Whoever was in here must have heard the car, and moved fast. When we walked in they'd gone, leaving the back door wide open. There was a roll of film on the table. Two frames had been exposed.'

'You got the film processed, and this photograph was one of them.' I touched the transparency lying on the table. 'But this is certainly not the other.'

'No. The two photographs were identical. I suppose the photographer was playing safe with exposure.' He hesitated, and I could imagine his mind replaying the moment.

'There was a camera on the table. An old Mamiya twin lens reflex I kept in a cupboard. And a Metz flashgun.'

I nodded. 'I was thinking Hasselblad — but you're saying they'd used your Mamiya?'

He wasn't listening. He picked up the transparency, holding it gingerly by the edges of the black mount. There was a tremor in his fingers.

'I've got a studio here,' he said. 'The garage was converted a long time ago. But I run the business from premises in Castle Street. There's a staff of three, and we use freelance photographers for weddings. But Danson Graphics is also a successful photo agency. We have a vast stock of transparencies.'

'Right. Businesses come to you when they need images for advertising, publicity . . . '

'Yes. All top quality medium format slides. Like this one.'

He paused, ran the back of a forefinger across the shiny surface of the transparency.

'I was in the office a week ago. My colleague, Graham Lee, was sorting stock. Ginny popped her head in, said she'd got something to show him. They went into the outer office. Then I heard Graham swear — and that was unusual. So I went through.'

Perspiration had dampened his forehead and upper lip like cold dew.

'There was a single transparency on Ginny's light box. The mail had arrived, and she was sorting through submissions.' He shook his head. 'Graham stepped in front of me, blocked my way. He said it was evil, sick, I shouldn't look. Ginny snatched it off the light box. I . . . had to force her to hand it over . . . '

Mutely, he handed it to me.

I held it up to the light, and felt the skin on my face tighten.

The same two men. Standing under the same oil painting. In the first photograph they'd been standing stiffly against the wall, like the masked men in those sinister videos released by hostage takers in Iraq. But in this transparency they were all over the place, clothes in disarray, struggling to hold two little boys in crumpled blue pyjamas who were fighting like wildcats. The men had their hands clamped over the boys' mouths. Sleeves had been pushed up; their muscular arms were like iron bands encircling bodies but failing to control thrashing arms, kicking legs. One little boy's pyjama top had been pushed up as he almost wriggled out of his captor's grasp. Soft flesh was exposed. Hard fingers dug in cruelly.

All right, it was a trannie. Nothing more than a square of film. But I swear that looking at it I could smell the masked men's sweat, hear the wet hiss of hot breath as the boys squirmed against the suffocating hands; I could feel the pounding of their young hearts, taste their terror . . .

And I was not their father; I had not had two sons snatched from me twenty years ago — so what in God's name was Frank Danson feeling?

'It came in like any other submission,' Danson said. 'But on the mount there's no name, no address. When I asked Ginny, she thought it might have been poked through the letter box by hand. But she couldn't be sure, because by that time the envelope had been ripped up and dumped.' His voice was expressionless. It was as if the words were uttered by a man carved out of dry wood.

'When I got home,' he said, 'there was . . . something else. Innocent in itself, but in the light of what had gone before . . . ' He smiled bitterly. 'Maybe I should coin a new phrase: in the *darkness* of what had gone before, it could have been painted in blood and coated with the stench of evil.'

4

'So what was this something else?'

Darkness had fallen. I was sitting in my favourite leather chair in Calum Wick's Grassendale flat. The only light was the Anglepoise over his work table. It shone on the furnishings, on the wide-screen television and Pioneer stereo system, on the wall where curling and faded blue-tacked photographs, newspaper cuttings and notebook jottings on torn pages displayed Calum Wick's wickedly subjective history of Liverpool.

Ten minutes earlier in the kitchen, watched unblinkingly by Satan, Calum's mauled black moggy, we'd polished off a Greek salad — feta cheese, tomatoes off the vine thinly sliced, olives, red onion and cucumber — and washed it down with Lazy Sunday coffee by Taylors of Harrogate. When we moved into the living-room my Scottish painter poured generous measures of the Macallan whisky over ice cubes jingling in crystal glasses, then listened as I ran swiftly through Frank Danson's story.

He was sprawled on the settee, long legs crossed at the ankles, paint-smeared Lennon glasses pushed up into his wiry hair. The smoke from the thin Schimmelpennick cigar he was holding swirled about his greying beard like clouds of dry ice around a fading rock star. Satan was asleep at his feet, head back, eyes shiny yellow slits.

Calum was watching me intently. He was waiting for the answer to his question.

'It was a card,' I said.

'The ace of spades? The Tarot's hanged man?'

'Neither of those — but bear with me while I add a little spice to the mixture.'

'A wee drop of mud to already murky waters.'

'You could be right. This afternoon a certain Welsh detective inspector invited me to gaze on the corpse of a man lying in dank woods. A little earlier Danny Maguire, the man who telephoned me the day after we closed the Sam Bone case, finally turned up. His wife is still missing. In conversation, he told me she had received a card in the mail.' I paused, cocked an eyebrow at Wick.

He grinned, waggled the cigar between his fingers.

'Even I, with my limited intelligence,' he said, 'can see where this is leading.'

'Mm. The two cards — Pat Maguire's and Danson's — bore different messages, but because of the timing it's likely that the same hand had done the writing. Written with a red felt pen. Pat Maguire got an order: *Remember to forget*. Danson got a clear statement: *The waiting is over*.'

'And he knew what that meant.'

'Yes. Twenty years ago, when Frank Danson's kids were taken, a similar card was left.'

'Let me guess,' Wick said. 'That one said *wait*.'

'Actually it was *Wait, Frankie, wait*. And at the time he couldn't understand the familiarity, because nobody had ever called him Frankie.'

'And what about Danny Maguire's wife? Did she also get a card twenty years ago? And if she did — or even if she didn't — what connects her to Danson?'

'I don't know. They've only been married eight years, so if there was one it was before his time. And we can't ask Mrs Maguire because, according to Danny, she's still missing.'

'Not dead?'

'Possibly. Her work puts her in close contact with criminals. And the corpse in the woods was Bill Fox, one of her male colleagues.'

'But if he's dead, and she's not, where is

she? On the run from the baddies?'

'Again, we don't know.'

Calum leaned across to rest the cigar in an ashtray, swung his legs off the settee, stood up and stretched. He took the paint-smeared glasses out of his hair and placed them on the work table alongside the rows of Light Dragoons, then went to stand in front of the wall plastered with cuttings. He scanned it swiftly, then came away stroking his beard.

'I thought there might've been something there. A newspaper cutting maybe — though probably not, and for good reason. The kiddies were snatched a wee bit before my time and yours; twenty years back we were both somewhere else.' He found the Macallan bottle, topped up the glasses. 'I know Danson from Night Owl — though not well. Bill Fox I've never heard of. Same with Maguire — until he phoned last week when we were debriefing in your kitchen.'

He grinned at the importance he'd bestowed on our amateur dabblings; picked up his glass, sipped, looked at me over the glittering rim.

'So what's the connection? What links these people? Danson. Fox. Mrs Maguire — '

'And Calvin Gay, the leader of a minor religious mission. He's connected to Pat

Maguire and Fox — and he almost certainly tells lies.'

'All right. Include him, and that's four. What's the link — and who the hell's playing nasty games with people's lives?'

I shrugged, watched as he shook his head and sat down at the work table. He poked with his forefinger at a Dragoon officer, touched the black helmet, the white metal crest and red mane. Looked at his finger and pulled a face, leaned closer to squint at the places he'd touched.

'You've told me what Danson told you,' he said, still looking for fingerprints, 'but was what Danson told you all there was to tell?'

'I'd say that what Danson told me was less important than what he left out. Because if we ignore links, corpses, lying religious cranks and women who take off into the wild blue yonder, we're left with one astonishing possibility, and a question we cannot answer.'

'What he left out was something he didn't dare put into words,' Calum said astutely. 'After twenty years, the astonishing possibility is that those two wee boys are alive.'

He carefully wiped the pad of his finger on a cloth damp with white spirit, left the work table and came to sit on the edge of the settee.

'And the unanswerable question,' I said, 'is

why, after all that time, is somebody out there telling Danson that the waiting is over?'

★ ★ ★

Some complicated problems are best left to the clever little men deep in our subconscious who work tirelessly through the dark night hours to unravel puzzles, make sense out of nonsense, and for our benefit inscribe their answers in neat bullet points on cerebral parchment. Calum had put the possibility into words Frank Danson was too terrified to utter, I had posed the unanswerable question, and that was where we left it. All-night discussions, I knew well, could too often result in brilliant deductions that in the cold light of dawn turn out to be wild flights of fancy.

It was gone midnight when I retired to the spare room. Satan was asleep in the kitchen. Calum was at his work table, brush in hand, light from the Anglepoise glinting on smeared glasses and a miniature Dragoon officer having his helmet touched up. At some time during the night I thought I heard him on the phone — Calum, not the officer. But I decided it was those clever little chaps twittering over the problem we'd dumped in their laps, and I felt myself smiling as I drifted off.

At breakfast the next morning, mouth full of toast, Calum asked the next obvious question.

'What do we do now?'

'Unless I was listening to birds twittering in the dark,' I said, 'I think you've taken the first step.'

'Yeah, I phoned late, caught up with Manny at Night Owl. He'll dig out some background info on the kidnapping.'

Manny Yates, the Lime Street PI and my mentor. A chubby character who wears waistcoats without jackets and takes liquid lunches in the American Bar, which is conveniently just a couple of doors down from his office.

'I was thinking,' I said, 'of visiting Haggard and Vine.'

'Waste of time.' He slotted bread into the toaster, poured coffee. 'Cops who've reached DI and DS now would have been bulling their boots in the Mather Avenue police academy when those kids were snatched.'

'They'll know where to look.'

'Aye, but what does Danson want?'

I pushed my plate away, leaned back with the coffee. 'We came to no firm arrangement. I think he's in six different minds, scared of rocking the boat.'

'But he prefers you to the police.'

'Mm.'

'So I'll toddle along and see Manny this morning.'

I opened my mouth — and my mobile rang.

It was in the living-room. I raced through and caught it on the fourth ring, listened to yet another unsteady voice then grunted as shock hit me like cold water.

'Yes, I understand, and of course I'll be there.'

Calum was leaning in the kitchen doorway, mug in hand, Satan like black smoke curling and purring against his leg.

'Get your coat,' I said. 'Frank Danson's got another photograph. It was delivered by hand, and from his voice I'd say it's another bombshell.'

5

Childwall Priory Road is a fifteen-minute drive from Grassendale, and I used that time to give Calum details of Danny Maguire's visit to Bryn Aur and the discovery of the corpse sprawled in eerie woods where lightning flickered and thundery rain pattered through the trees to form a fine mist that left us soaked and miserable.

He shook his head when I'd finished, and just had time to suggest that Welshman DI Alun Morgan would have lapped up every minute of the crappy weather before I swung the Quatro into Danson's gravel drive and slithered to a halt.

A different time of day from my first visit and the morning sun had not yet reached the living-room. October, and quite cool. Danson offered us coffee, which we refused. I introduced Calum Wick. We sat in chairs flanking the coffee table. My business card was there. So was the transparency and the square of white paper I knew was a 5″ × 5″ print from a twenty-year-old medium format negative.

But now there was also a second transparency.

Danson paced between table and window, window and roll-top desk. I studied his face, searching for grief.

What I saw was barely suppressed excitement, and I knew the astonishing possibility Calum and I had discussed was moving towards a probability. But not yet there. The excitement was being suppressed because Danson still wasn't one hundred percent certain that his boys were alive. Which suggested that the latest photograph was . . . what? Encouraging, but inconclusive?

'Can I see? And the card you got with the earlier delivery?'

Danson snapped a look at me, nodded, and went across the room. He found the card on the desk, handed it to me, moved away again to stare out of the rear window.

The writing *was* unusual. Done with red felt pen. Somewhere between printing and joined up writing but not quite either.

The waiting is over

I put the card down. My hand hovered over the images. It was like the three-card trick, with no winners. The photograph of two masked men posing for a portrait I passed to Calum. I picked up one of the transparencies, again felt something inside me turn cold and sad as I looked at two pyjama-clad little boys squirming in the grip of evil men; felt that same ice begin to melt in a way that could easily lead to tears as I passed the transparency to Calum and held the second transparency up to the light.

I'm no expert at judging age, but I guessed the two boys playing on the sloping lawns were five or six. If they were Danson's kids, this photograph must have been taken two or three years after the snatch. It was impossible for me to recognize them. All I had to go by was the image of much younger boys with black gloved hands clamped over their faces. I had seen only their terrified, staring eyes.

'Definitely them?' I said, and Danson came away from the window.

'I'd say so. But how would I know?' His smile was twisted, ugly. 'Those are not my kids in that picture, are they? By the time that was taken they belonged to somebody else, someone with a big house in the country, someone — '

He broke off. Ran fingers through his mop of white hair.

I sighed, put down the transparency and watched a wooden-faced Calum Wick do the same with the images he had been studying.

'Can you do prints of these?'

Danson looked at me and nodded. 'I'll take

them into work, use the scanner.'

'Print off a couple of each. Ten by eights.'

He scooped them up, squared them, slumped into a chair.

'We did some thinking last night,' I said, 'and came up with a possibility and a question — not very clever of us, because I'm sure you've got there already. The possibility — made more likely by this latest offering — is that your boys are alive. The *question* is, why has somebody decided to tell you the waiting is over.'

'Yes, both *have* occurred to me,' Danson said drily. 'I hardly dare contemplate one, and can't answer the other — and there's also the obvious third question that's been tormenting me ever since that night: who the hell is the sadistic bastard behind this?'

'Twenty years buries a lot of secrets,' I said, and instantly regretted my choice of words. 'For the answers to those questions we need to go all the way back to the beginning, and start digging.'

Danson looked at the face down photographs, shuddered, and sprang out of the chair. He'd been holding up well, but seemed suddenly unable to bear the atmosphere in a room that held so many memories.

'For God's sake let's get out of here, do our talking in the studio.'

He led the way through the kitchen to a rear passageway, then through a connecting door into the double garage and switched on the light. It was an excellent conversion, clearly well used, equipped with overhead lighting and studio electronic flash, rolls of coloured backdrop material on high stands, tripods, metal lockers, trestle tables and stacked chairs.

'I used to do landscapes as a respite from the business down town,' he said, 'but I'm getting too old to lug medium format gear ten miles across rugged terrain in time to catch a misty dawn. We do run landscape comps on our web site. One's running now, with a nice cash prize for some lucky amateur and guaranteed exposure on the site.' He shrugged. 'But I'm getting off the track . . . '

'The in thing nowadays is digital, isn't it?'

'Oh, yes. The changeover's been done at Danson Graphics. I'll never go back.'

'But we will,' I said. 'We *must*, however painful,' and he acknowledged that with a reluctant nod of the head.

With a clatter, Calum lifted three chairs from the stack and handed them around.

'Let's look at motive,' I said, sitting down and turning to Danson as he took the third chair. 'Twenty years ago, someone walked into your house and took your two young sons. Why?'

'They wanted the boys, someone else wanted the boys — or someone wanted to hurt me.'

I nodded. 'All right. Let's assume from the photograph of them playing in a garden that somebody wanted the boys; that a family wanted them, probably a childless family. Taking them was the easy bit. But then what?'

'Aye,' Calum said. 'A kidnapping like that would be on the front pages of all the national newspapers, with photographs. How could a childless family explain the sudden appearance of two small boys? Boys matching the photograph of your missing bairns. And what about birth certificates, medical records and so on?'

'Criminals have ways,' Danson said.

'That's true,' I said. 'And a family who paid to have children kidnapped would already be dealing with criminals, and have the cash to buy false identity documents.'

'I'm not convinced,' Calum said. 'I would definitely lean towards the other option.'

'All right.' I looked at Danson. 'So what about enemies? Who hated you so much they'd take your children to cause you pain?'

'Nobody.'

'What about your wife?'

'No.'

'There may be something she hasn't told you.'

'If that's the case, we're too late,' Danson said, and there was such desolation in his voice it seemed that the studio turned chill. 'Jenny's been dead for more than twenty years. A year after the boys were taken she went into the bathroom, lit a perfumed candle and switched off the light. Then she stripped, climbed into a hot bath with a bottle of wine and a glass. She drank half of it, lying back in the hot suds. When she was pleasantly muzzy, she slit both her wrists with a Stanley knife.' His legs were crossed. One foot was rapidly jiggling. 'I'm making some of that up,' he said, 'because I knew her so well and because she'd told me that, if missing the boys became too awful to bear, that's what she'd do.' He paused. The silence was awful. 'I was downstairs,' he said, 'watching television. I kicked the bathroom door open when time passed and she wouldn't answer my call. When I saw the bottle, a cog must have slipped in my brain because for a moment I thought she'd been bathing in red wine . . . ' His short laugh was chilling. 'But then I realized the water was red with her blood . . . '

'I'm so sorry,' I said.

'It's all right. You couldn't know.' He shook his head, and I could hear the ghosts of memory twittering as they fled into the dark recesses where they lurked. 'But to answer your question,' he said, 'no, she had no enemies. Jenny was universally loved.'

For a few moments we sat doing nothing except replay in our minds scenes that were too appalling for Calum and me to imagine, too etched in Frank Danson's memory ever to be erased.

'Peter and Michael were taken for a reason,' I said at last. 'If it would be enormously difficult for two kidnapped boys to be assimilated into a family, and you and your wife had no enemies — what other reason could there be?'

I was looking at Frank Danson as I spoke, and I knew we weren't going to get much more. He had taken us with him to his photographic studio when the living-room was no longer bearable but, after twenty years of relative peace, raw memories had been exposed by events and now they were hounding him and in that house there was nowhere to hide.

Calum had read the same signs and gave me a warning look. I nodded.

Danson said, 'The only other possibility was a random snatch, or' — he swallowed

— 'a random double killing. But the police ruled that out. The random bit, I mean. Because the planning was fiendishly clever and suggested . . . '

He trailed off, frowning. There was sudden anger sparking in his eyes.

'Go on,' I said. 'What did it suggest?'

He took a deep breath. 'The way it was worked suggested someone had intimate knowledge of my family.'

Calum stood up. I knew he was itching to get details of that clever planning, but he could see that Danson was running out of steam. So he said, almost as an aside, 'Intimate knowledge suggests relatives, or close friends.' He waited. 'Somebody who knew you as Frankie, not Frank.'

Danson shook his head. 'No such person existed. I've always been Frank.'

I said, 'Were any of your relatives or close friends investigated by the police?'

'No.'

Danson blurted the word. Too quickly, I thought. And now his eyes were dull, his face drawn. He looked at me and came slowly out of the plastic chair like a tired old man after a long wait at the surgery.

'The police,' he said, 'came up with nothing. It was always a dead end. There were no suspects.'

'He was lying,' Calum said.

'He's asked me to help him, and he's going to pay me — I think. So why would he lie?'

I was driving back to Grassendale. It was eleven o'clock, I had the taste of Bell's whisky in my mouth and I was looking forward to strong, unlaced coffee.

'Because you proved more perceptive than he'd expected. And all is not straightforward: he has something to hide.'

I smiled. 'Mm. He started down a trail, realized what he was doing, didn't like what he might have to tell me and backed off.'

'That business about intimate knowledge of the family was infuriating him,' Calum said. 'I wonder why? Too bloody close to home for comfort?'

'It sounds as if somebody near and dear has some explaining to do.'

'Any ideas?'

'The only person he mentioned to me,' I said, as I took the turning that brought the Quatro to the parking place in front of Wick's flat, 'was his wife's sister. She was their usual babysitter. That night she was miles away, in Scotland.'

Calum climbed out. He was standing on the grass verge looking at the sun glittering on the flat waters of the Mersey when I joined him.

'So who did the honours?'

'A young girl. The Dansons drove to the theatre, changed their minds and rushed home. When they got there, the house was empty.'

'Childwall to town, and back,' Calum said. 'What's that, half an hour, forty-five minutes?'

'No more,' I said. 'The fiendish planning obviously called for a quick in and out; the kidnappers couldn't possibly have known the Dansons would return early.'

We were climbing the stairs. Calum brushed past me, keys jingling. He said, 'What baffles me is how, in that short time, they not only snatched the kids but somehow first managed to get past the baby-sitter.'

But I was no longer listening.

He'd opened the door to his flat and now, mingling tantalizingly with the familiar smells of white spirit, Humbrol enamel paints and Schimmelpennick cigars, there was a faint perfume I would have detected instantly after a week spent living in a reeking septic tank sharing a diet of garlic bread with a skunk.

In her usual maddening, lovable, unexpected way, Sian Laidlaw had come home.

6

Perhaps 'coming home' was laying it on a bit thick, because for Sian Laidlaw the concept has always been a little unreal. This, after all, is a woman who had seen her Scottish seafaring father lost overboard in an Arctic gale when she'd been ten years old and illegally aboard his ship, had returned to nurse her dying mother in the Cardiff slums and, years later, with a university degree under her Shotokan karate black belt, moved north to become something of a legend among the high peaks of the Cairngorms.

I had met her in Norway — she taking a break from military duty, me on holiday and stepping gingerly onto skis for the first time since my own stint in uniform. Some months after that first meeting she had walked one day into my stone workshop at Bryn Aur and in the next two years had shared my home and occasionally my bed — I liked to think the initiative was always mine, but that's just the crowing of the macho male that lurks within every man.

If I liked or used the word relationship I'd say the one Sian and I had was on and off

— God forbid, I might even have called her my partner! But whatever name we gave to what we did have, we worked at it. After a spell instructing on an outward bound course for tired executives in storm-force winds at Cape Wrath — this long after she had quit the army — she had returned to Liverpool and helped me with the Gault case but, behind the scenes, other more attractive propositions were looming. After Cape Wrath she had conducted a successful radio phone-in. That led to the offer of her own television series, to be filmed by Granada in Manchester. We were delighted, Sian anticipating less time spent in the field teaching overgrown office boys how to abseil down vertical cliff faces, me looking forward to more togetherness at Bryn Aur.

In a way it had worked out. We *did* spend more time together. But then the Sam Bone case took over, drew to a bloody close in Conwy harbour, and Sian was again called to Manchester to discuss another series — this time overseas. And so I found myself nursing a gunshot wound at Bryn Aur without my Soldier Blue; without knowing if the next time I saw her she'd be sporting a heavy tan under a dusty hat with corks dangling from the brim as she merrily dished out souvenir Koala key-rings.

But she was unchanged, eyes like deep mountain lakes, hair like corn, jeans and sweater tight enough to make a strong man's throat ache, perfume — sniffed from close range when we embraced — so tantalizing the room swam and I had to cling to her for support.

She leaned back in my arms and smiled with mock sympathy.

'You're weaker — and you look *old*,' she said.

'A week has passed,' I said with dignity. 'I'm a *little* older.'

'Mm,' she said, smirking. 'So'm I — but on you, it shows.'

'I take it you got the sack.'

She chuckled. 'Old, but perceptive. And why am I taking it out on you when it's that bastard Nigel who wants castrating?'

'Wants?'

'Needs. His influence got the second series put on hold. The Galapagos Islands are not for me.'

'The Lord be praised,' Calum Wick said, heading for the kitchen.

'Ah,' Sian said. 'You boys are battling with baddies again.'

'On two fronts,' I said. 'Or perhaps not.'

'Isn't it always like that?' Sian said. 'With you and crime, one thing always leads to another — except when it doesn't.'

'This time,' I said, 'the links are so obvious it's uncanny. It's finding out what the links link that's proving difficult.'

'Early days,' Calum called, now rattling cups and running water.

'And of course Jack'll tell me all about it,' she said, 'over coffee.'

So I did. I was expecting something bland, but the coffee Calum eventually carried through smelt remarkably like expensive brandy, its effect had very little to do with caffeine, and by the time I'd worked my way from the corpse in the woods to Danny Maguire's missing wife and the heart-wrenching tale of Danson's two kidnapped boys, it was midday and we were mellow.

And reflective.

'The relaxed brain produces ideas,' I said, 'the way a sturgeon produces eggs.'

'Confuciusly,' Sian said, and giggled.

'Aye, but how many of those eggs,' Calum said, 'turn into another wee sturgeon?'

'Spoilsport,' Sian said, pouting. She sipped coffee thoughtfully, looked at me enquiringly.

'We know the dead man is linked to Maguire's wife,' she said. 'But that case is being looked at by Alun Morgan — right?'

'Right.'

'So leaving that investigation in his capable

hands, let's consider those cards with their red writing. They *must* link Maguire's wife to Frank Danson, now, and in the past. You're working for Danson, whose boys were kidnapped twenty years ago. To help him, the first thing you should do is look at that connection.'

'No good asking Danson, he's worn out,' I said, and Calum nodded. 'He's waiting for another envelope to flop through the door, and he's scared stiff it's going to be bad news. I think it'll be more useful talking to Maguire.'

'Do it now,' Sian said, and smiled sweetly.

I dug out my mobile phone, found the paper on which I'd scrawled Maguire's number, punched the right buttons in the right order.

He must have been waiting by the phone — if his wife was still missing I could understand why.

'Any news?' I said.

'Nothing.'

'That's good, surely?'

He snorted noisily.

'Tell me,' I said, 'Have you thought any more about that card your wife got?'

'No — why?'

'A man I'm doing some PI work for has also received one. Going by what you told me, they sound identical but bear different messages. Which means there's almost certainly some kind of connection between your wife and this man. But it's not quite that simple. My nameless client got a card exactly like these twenty years ago. That first one told him to wait. This one — as you'd expect if you follow the logic — tells him the waiting's over.'

There was silence at the other end of the phone. Calum and Sian were watching me over their coffee mugs. I waited. Suddenly thought of something, and felt a surge of excitement.

'If you're asking me if my wife got a similar card twenty years ago,' Maguire said, 'I can't tell you. We've been together ten years. That's some way short.'

'Your wife's first name's Pat. Is that Pat as in Patricia?'

'Yes — but so what?'

'I'm not sure,' I said, lying through my teeth. 'It's something I thought of that might lead somewhere. Then again, it might mean nothing.'

But his mind was elsewhere. He said, 'I haven't had any news, but what about you? Have you spoken to that Welsh detective?'

'I'm going to. I'll ask if he's made progress.'

I was about to break the connection, but

Sian was waving urgently.

'Ask him about kids,' she said softly. 'Has he got any?'

I frowned, not understanding. She waved me on.

I said into the phone, 'This may sound like a strange question, but I've been prompted to ask you if you have any children.'

'By the police?'

'A colleague.'

'Tell him the answer's yes.'

I nodded at Sian. She mouthed, 'How old?'

'What are they now?' I said. 'Seven, eight?'

'No, Pat's two, Danny's three.' He laughed awkwardly. 'Some parents. Late starters, no imagination.'

'But two lovely kids, I'm sure,' I said. 'Make sure you look after them.'

And I broke the connection before he could ask why.

'Christ!' I said. 'Where the hell did you get that from?'

Sian would have looked smug if my face hadn't told her how hitting the nail on the head cranked up the danger.

'I could put the same question to you,' she said. 'Why'd you ask him his wife's name?'

'We're talking about links, and I remembered the babysitter. Danson told me her name was Tricia. Now Maguire's told me his

52

wife's name's Patricia. She's got a card that links her to Danson. So guess where she was on a certain night twenty years ago.'

'Baby-sitting. And how old are Maguire's kids now?'

'Two and three.'

Sian shook her head ruefully. 'It was a shot in the dark. Pat Maguire got a card through the post, and she's disappeared. But the card in itself is no threat. So I figured if she is linked to Danson, then any threat is something she's recognized from the past. If you're right, and she was the baby-sitter, then, yes, she might believe her children are being threatened.'

'But why walk out on them?' Calum said. 'Wouldn't a mother want to be with her bairns?'

'They're being threatened *because* of her,' Sian said. 'She's distancing herself from them.'

'Threatened because she knows something,' I said. 'Something happened when she was baby-sitting. She was *there*, in the house looking after the kids, so she must have seen *something*.' I shrugged. 'But the only person who can tell me if I'm right — other than the police who questioned her at the time — is Manny Yates.'

'Aye, and we'll get around to Manny,'

Calum said. 'But, to my way of thinking, the people threatening Pat Maguire could be fretting that she's down at some nick spilling the beans. If that's the case, then the obvious thing to do is snatch her kids anyway to shut her up.'

Sian was biting her lip. 'Maybe,' she said, 'we're jumping to conclusions, taking what Danny Maguire's told us at face value. What if Pat Maguire didn't walk out? What if she's already been taken?'

I shook my head in disgust. 'We don't know enough, do we? Let's go and talk to Manny.'

'We'll all go,' Sian said, springing to her feet and gathering the empty mugs. 'But, Jack, ring Alun Morgan first.'

I caught the Welsh DI in his Bethesda office.

'Alun,' I said, 'anything new on the body?'

'Ah, well now, that would depend, wouldn't it?'

'On what.'

'On which one you mean.'

I waited. So did Alun, probably with macabre glee. I said, 'Go on, enlighten me.'

'When you left there was just the one causing problems. Now there's two.'

I took a deep breath. 'Pat Maguire?'

'That's it, yes. Her Suzuki had been driven into the woods flanking Llyn Elsi. She was

54

lying on the back seat.'

'Damn!'

'Before you phone your Mr Maguire with the tragic news, I can tell you Merseyside police officers are on there way there now.' He paused. 'And, while you are on the phone, there's something else that might interest you.'

'Not another body?'

'Indeed. It seems your Liverpool low life has taken to looking after its own in a peculiar way. A middle-aged scally was moved from prison to a cosy hospital bed, and that's where he died. And a couple of hours after he died, the body was nicked. It was there, and then it wasn't, and the mortuary at the Royal Liverpool is now trying to explain how a man recently deceased managed to climb off the slab and walk out into the cold.'

7

'I can't believe it,' Sian said. 'One minute Maguire's listening to you telling him there's no news, the next he'll be answering the door to the police who'll tell him his wife's dead.'

'Who's this James Cagan?' Calum said.

'Small-time crook. Age forty-five. He was taken ill in prison and moved to the hospital. He died a week ago.'

Sian narrowed her eyes. 'There's only one reason I can see for Alun telling you about Cagan. A week ago is when the cards with their sinister messages began arriving and Pat Maguire disappeared. She may be dead, but she's still an important link, isn't she?'

'According to Alun,' I said, 'there was only one person with Cagan when he died. A woman.'

'All right,' Calum said with feigned weariness, 'out with the bloody theories.'

'Pat Maguire visited dangerous criminals in prison. We know that. But according to Danny, she continued to see them when they're released.'

'Or get sick and end up in intensive care,' Sian said. 'Do you think the woman at

56

Cagan's bedside was Pat Maguire?'

'It's a possibility.'

Calum was up and slipping his feet into light tan Timberland boots.

'Unfortunately,' he said, 'if *that's* a possibility then we can really go wild with conjecture and assume James Cagan is now an ingredient in the evil brew we've been stirring. I mean, good God, we've got every man and his dog linked to a kidnapping that happened twenty years ago — so why not Cagan?' He shrugged into his leather jacket. 'And tell me,' he said, 'why has nobody spent a few minutes considering Bill Fox's role in this? The poor man was murdered for a reason. And he's been pretty close to Pat Maguire. Are we not going to consider him for a starring role?'

I said, 'Are you going somewhere?'

'I,' he said, 'am swanning down town to pick a crafty fat man's brains. Wasn't that the general idea before the bodies started piling up?'

★   ★   ★

Whenever I stamp my way up the brown-linoleumed stairs into Manny Yates's dusty Lime Street office it's as if I'm stepping back in time. There's no blackboard, no scarred

57

wooden desks with hinged lids and carved initials, but my mind is always swamped by memories of damp macs, Wellingtons, disinfectant, crates of milk in small bottles warming by radiators and an all-pervading, dusty ambience that suggests tight-strung cellos and yellowing pages of pianoforte on tall music stands, ledges thick with chalk dust, and always books, books, books.

But this is not primary school. This small room with its desks and banker's green-shaded lights and filing cabinets and cork boards with coloured pins and portable electric heaters is where I served my private eye apprenticeship — albeit at the ripe old age of thirty-five — and so the memories of monumental cock ups (which always seemed to outnumber the triumphs) prevail as they come swooping back to mock and gibber, and by the time I'm halfway across the room to Manny's desk I'm reduced to a shivering wreck.

Well, it makes a good story, doesn't it!

In truth, Manny Yates has always put me at ease. My no nonsense overweight mentor, sitting at his desk with his red waistcoat's buttons straining to keep its edges together, a thin Schimmelpennick cigar smouldering between wet lips, black eyes twinkling with amusement and a white scalp glistening like a fish's belly through a threadbare comb-over that would have had a younger Bobby Charlton green with envy.

'Grab some chairs,' he said, as we trooped in. 'If you want drinks, Jack knows where they're hid.' He grinned toothily around the cigar. 'He used to be my office boy — did he tell you?'

'The way he tells it, his status gets somewhat elevated,' Calum Wick said.

He spun one of the two available wooden chairs around for Sian, grabbed the other for himself and grinned across at me.

'I'll pace up and down nervously,' I said. 'And you can forget about drinks. Clear heads are needed. You two puff nonchalantly at your cigars.'

'And I,' said Sian, 'will try not to laugh.'

'Right, Manny,' I said, casting a glance out of the window at the streams of traffic coursing along Lime Street then swinging back to confront him. 'What did you dig up on the Danson story?'

'No diggin' necessary.' He tapped his shiny brow. 'Most of it's in 'ere.'

He leaned sideways. I heard a waistcoat button pop as he pulled open a drawer. His face was red from the effort as he straightened and dropped a manila folder on the desk.

'There's cuttin's in there if they're needed, but first tell me what you've got so we don't waste time.'

I sat down on the window sill, felt the draught from the open sash window on my neck and began relating the twenty-year-old story. When I'd finished, he nodded.

'That was then, an' most of it was in the *Echo*. So what's new?'

'Now Danson's been sent another card. *The waiting is over*. Two more photographs over a couple of days. The first shows those two men holding the struggling youngsters. Mere babes. The next shows two boys a couple of years older, playing in the garden of a large country house. That one hurt Danson. He recognized them, and now knows they were alive a couple of years after they were taken. So for him the waiting's not over — and I don't suppose the irony is lost on the perpetrators — it's started all over again.'

'An' you've got a lot more, no doubt,' Manny said. 'Because Danson's been doin' this talkin' an' you've been diggin' an' I'd guess you've been jumpin' to wild conclusions.'

'That's sort of the way an investigation takes off,' Calum said. 'But it's wild *conjecture* first, leading eventually to logical conclusions.'

60

'Mm.' I nodded agreement. 'Trouble is even conjecture's proving difficult. That's all Danson gave us, so we've got more questions than answers.'

'That's always been the way with the Danson case,' Manny said. 'So what do *you* think's goin' on? — if wild conjecture's not beyond you.'

'Someone's out there, of course,' I said. 'The new message — *the waiting is over* — could have been written by any cruel person who followed the original case and wants to cause mischief. But the new photographs with that message seem to guarantee it's the kidnapper — and we're short of suspects.'

'The police came up with three before givin' up,' Manny said.

'I can manage two,' Calum said. 'The baby-sitter, and Danson because he's one of the parents.' He thought for a moment. 'That means I have to include Jenny, Danson's wife, even though she committed suicide a year later. That could have been remorse. So, yes, that's three.'

'Not bad for amateurs,' Manny said, and he dropped his dead cigar into an ashtray. He licked his lips. Looked pointedly at Sian. She looked at me. Then she got up, went to a heavy wooden filing cabinet, found a bottle of cheap whisky and a glass in the top drawer and brought them to Manny.

He poured a drink. Drank. Looked at me. I shook my head.

'Yeah,' Manny said, sitting back, 'the obvious one was the baby-sitter. She was twenty-two, fresh out of university and about to start a gap year in Australia. An' she was supposed to be lookin' after the kids but wasn't there when the Dansons got home.'

'But the police found her?'

'Sure. She was at home with her mum.'

'And?'

'First, answer me this one: where was the sister, the regular baby-sitter?'

I frowned. 'According to Frank Danson, she was at a police conference in Scotland.'

'Yeah, that's right. Her name's Becky Long. Still is, 'cos she's never married. At the time she was a DI. And she was unavailable because she was three hundred miles away. But — accordin' to Tricia when she was questioned — shortly after the Dansons left there was a ring at the bell, she opened the door, and a fair-haired woman smiled merrily at her and walked straight in.' Manny sipped his drink. Let the tension mount. 'She said she was Becky Long. The cop. An' she waltzed on into the livin'-room, told Tricia there was no point two of them bein' there so she was takin' over the baby-sittin'.'

'Bloody hell,' Sian said.

'Tricia was a sensible kid. She protested. The woman was unfazed — '

'The sister,' I said.

'Hang on. This *woman* said Tricia could check her identity if she was doubtful; in the main bedroom she'd find a photograph of her on holiday with her sister. Which bore the unmistakable ring of honesty and truth, so Tricia was already teetering. An' then the woman said, if Tricia felt *really* guilty, she could ease her conscience by leaving the money she'd been paid on the coffee table on her way out.'

'Clever,' Sian said. 'How much was it?'

'Twenty quid from Frank Danson. The woman made it up to thirty — said she deserved more, 'specially as she was goin' on a gap year to Oz.'

'So Tricia left?' I said.

'Nine out of ten would've done,' Manny said. 'The woman walked in like she owned the place. She knew Tricia's name. Knew about the gap year.'

'And there was a photograph of her upstairs,' Calum said — and looked at Manny.

'Yeah,' Manny said. 'Only there wasn't.'

Calum tugged thoughtfully at his beard.

'But Becky Long *did* confirm that she was at the conference in Scotland?'

'Er, no, she couldn't,' Manny said.

I looked at him, waiting. He lit another cigar. Puffed smoke.

I said, 'Why the hell not?'

'She was havin' a feud with a superior officer who was blockin' her promotion. He was takin' early retirement, and still had his knife into her. So she walked out of the conference a day early, handed in her notice a week later.'

'Good for her,' Sian said. 'But even if she left early, she would have an alibi.'

'No,' Manny said. 'She didn't.'

'But the girl, Tricia,' I said, 'could confirm that the real Becky Long was not the woman who walked into the Dansons' house.'

'No, she couldn't, not for definite.'

'Oh, come on,' I said, 'why the hell not?'

'Think about it. Tricia saw the woman in the Dansons' house for five minutes max. It took the police a week to bring her and Becky Long together. The girl was flyin' to Australia the next day, half her mind was on the other side of the world. The woman who'd impersonated Becky — if that's the way it was — had done her homework. I mean, if she knew all about Tricia, she'd know about Becky, what she looked like.' He shrugged. 'If

64

she was the same height and build — an' Becky was medium, not too tall, not too short — she could pull on a blonde wig, splash on some make-up . . . '

'There's another possibility,' I said. 'Maybe the baby-sitter was got at in that week. Threatened. Warned off.'

I eased myself off the window sill, rubbed the back of my neck. The skin was cold. The chill wasn't all from the draught.

I said, 'When we were looking for Gerry Gault, the big question was, where is he? The puzzle when we were chasing after Jason Bone was, why did he order a Mercedes, then disappear?' I shook my head in the silence. 'The question here is, why *now*? Why, after twenty years, is the waiting over? And if it is the kidnapper or kidnappers who have come crawling out of the woodwork, what exactly is it everyone's been waiting for?'

★　★　★

The meeting in Manny Yates's office broke up, Sian heading for Allerton Road where she had an appointment with an estate agent (news to me — and worrying), Calum to Renshaw Street where he'd be picked up by Stan Jones in his rusty white van and transported to an unspecified location, there

65

to hatch devious plots for imminent inventive scams.

And yet, I couldn't be sure. He'd been acting strangely of late, Calum Wick. There was nothing I could pin down and say, ah, so that's what's wrong, but there really was something odd and that led me to believe he was engaged in more than just another money-making scheme.

With Manny I took the short walk along Lime Street to the American Bar. There, over an ice-cold bitter shandy, I told him about the death of Bill Fox, about Danny Maguire and the wife who had gone missing and now also been found dead and the possible connections to a sort of prisoners' aid mission in Woolton run by an American, and the news from Alun Morgan that a body had been stolen from the Royal Liverpool hospital.

That last bit amused him, but left him puzzled.

My next disclosure — that Maguire's dead wife had recently received a card similar to Danson's telling her to *Remember to forget* and that she was almost certainly Tricia, the baby-sitter — left him mildly interested, but impressed him not at all.

'So what?' he said. 'If she's dead, where does that get you? Apart from leavin' you minus one suspect. I mean, as a young kid

66

she never was a likely kidnapper, was she.'

But then I told him that Patricia Maguire had been linked to the Woolton mission, had dealt with criminals both in prison and out on the streets, and that the body stolen from the Royal Liverpool was that of James Cagan, a known, small-time crook.

'And there was a woman with him when he died,' I said. 'That was a week ago. And it was about a week ago that those blunt messages flopped through letter boxes, and Patricia Maguire went missing.'

That got his attention. He was puffing on a cigar, flicking ash off his waistcoat and drinking a double Bells with ice. His eyes narrowed.

'So where's it leadin'? You think Pat Maguire, the baby-sitter, was also the woman at the hospital?'

'That's all it is, a thought.'

'An' what then? Cagan had something to do with the kidnapping, or what?'

'I don't know.'

'Even if he did have, he's dead — and now Danson's had another photograph.'

'Yes. But both photographs show *two* masked men.'

'Yeah, right. An' if we can believe the baby-sitter's story we know for sure a woman was involved, don't we? Probably let the two men into the house.' He puffed on his cigar, face glistening through the haze. 'So the woman watchin' Cagan fall off his perch could've been the Becky Long impersonator, couldn't it? The third kidnapper. I mean, why Tricia Maguire? Twenty years ago, as baby-sitter, she just happened to be in the wrong place.'

'Unless she was a plant,' I said. 'Put there for the critical half-hour. Someone willing to make a few quid to let the other woman into the house. In that case she'd know too much — which would explain the warning card.'

Manny rocked his head from side to side, pulling a face, not convinced. 'Yeah, maybe; could be that's what she was. But that still makes her a bit player, in and out, job done — and I still reckon the woman at Cagan's bedside *could've* been the woman who walked into Danson's house twenty years ago.'

'Yes,' I said. 'But ultimately I could be reading too much into those hospital visits. As far as I know Cagan was nothing more than a small-time thief. So maybe, after all, it was just Cagan's tearful, white-haired old mother, weeping at the bedside of her dying son who's sole claim to fame was he got caught stealing ladies' knickers off clotheslines.'

8

I left Manny in the American Bar with his shirt sleeves rolled up as he talked business with a detective I had seen when I'd been summoned to the Admiral Street nick during the Sam Bone case. Sight of him reminded me that I really should discuss the Danson case with DI Mike Haggard and his DS sidekick, Willie Vine. As Calum had pointed out, they were unlikely to have information readily available on such an old case, but a sensible private eye keeps his connections within the police force gently simmering. If they go off the boil — or boil over because the detectives sense a deliberate affront — then the PI becomes an ex-PI because he's out in the cold.

However, my priority was checking on the woman who'd been with James Cagan at the Royal.

I'd parked the Quatro in the Mount Pleasant high rise. At that time of day the drive to Mossley Hill took less than twenty minutes. Danny Maguire lived in Carnatic Road. He was at home. I had expected a grief-stricken man with red eyes and grey face. There was none of that. He listened to my commiserations without seeming to hear them. When I told him the investigation I was on would almost certainly lead me to his wife's killer, the look in his eyes was something close to amusement.

What the hell was I seeing? A man guilty of murdering his wife. Or someone so deeply in shock that reality had gone fluttering out of the window?

He agreed readily when I asked for a photograph of his dead wife. Although he didn't say so, I knew he was wondering why I'd left the request for so long.

I thanked him for his help, drove back up the hill and onto Rose Lane. Fifteen minutes later my car was in the hospital car-park and I was on my way up to the ICU.

I spoke to a junior nurse, and was directed to a ward sister. She was at the nurses' station, filling in forms. She sat back when I told her what I wanted. Her hair was mussed, her face pink. I think she found paperwork a pain in the neck.

'Yes,' she said. 'I was on duty when James Cagan died.'

'And there was a woman with him?'

She nodded. 'He was here six days. She came in every afternoon, and stayed for hours.'

'When was he brought in? And when did he die?'

'It's now, what, Tuesday the 11th. He died a week last Friday — the 30th of September. He was brought in the Saturday before that — the 24th.' She was leaning forward, flicking through papers on a clipboard.

Maguire had telephoned me about his wife's disappearance at the end of the Sam Bone affair. That was a Sunday, October the 2nd. If there *were* connections, then the person who had murdered Bill Fox and Pat Maguire had moved fast once Cagan had snuffed it.

'He was brought in more than ten days ago, and died six days later. So when did his body go walkabout?'

She shook her head. 'I'm sorry. I really can't talk about that. Not unless you're from the police.'

I smiled. 'I'm not. What about the woman, then? Was she a friend, relative?'

'His sister.'

'You're sure?'

'No. But she *said* she was. He was single, she was too young to be his mother and she kept him company even if he wasn't too aware of what was going on . . . ' She shrugged.

I took out the photograph of Patricia

Maguire, placed it on the desk.

'Is that her?'

She looked at it and shook her head. 'No. Nothing like her.'

'So what *was* she like?'

'Shortish dark hair, streaked with grey. Age, not fashion. Medium everything: height, build, voice, looks.'

'Insignificant?'

She smiled and twiddled her pen. 'I suppose. And tired-looking, like most nurses.'

'But she wasn't a nurse?'

'I couldn't say. She could have been a brain surgeon. Or a detective, the way she sat there; she had one of those micro-cassette record-ers. She could have been anything at all — but she *said* she was Cagan's sister.'

Which, on reflection, seemed to rule out my suggestion to Manny that the woman at Cagan's bedside was his mother. Cagan had died in middle-age. His mother could have been sixty, and nowadays many sixty-year-olds wear designer leisure gear and look twenty years younger. But very few of them would carry micro-cassette recorders to pick up their dying son's last words.

I left the ward sister to her mind-numbing paperwork and wended my way through linoleumed passages that led to healthy open air, vast expanses of oil-stained concrete and my car. There I sat for a few moments watching visitors and outpatients plodding to and fro while I considered my next move.

To put life into a sluggish investigation there seemed to be two courses open to me. Either I started from the present and worked back, or started twenty years ago and worked forward. Or were both those routes identical? The two people definitely involved in the kidnapping — and reachable without too much digging — were Frank Danson and his wife's sister, Becky Long. They were there twenty years ago, still here now; by talking to either of them I would be jumping the gap between past and present.

The quickest way to Becky Long was through Frank Danson.

I pulled out of the car-park, made my way to the Paradise Street high rise and from there walked up the hill to turn right into Castle Street. The town hall was facing me at the far end, Danson Graphics in the middle of the block on the left behind windows of expensive smoked glass. Colours seen through them were muted shades of pastel, human skin turned to putty. I pushed in through a door that announced my presence with a sound like those periodic pings you hear on holiday charter flights, and suddenly I was in warmth and light where pink and yellow silk flowers stood in tall floor vases, carpet tiles muffled footsteps, three desks created an island of space where clients could be greeted, and some kind of noiseless air-conditioning kept the temperature balmy and subtly perfumed.

I thought of smelly melting pots and molten metal in a stone workshop, gloved hands holding a smoking-hot ladle, and wondered — not for the first time — if making toy soldiers was the wrong job.

Beyond the desks, in a shaded area, a man sat at a desk with white light shining eerily upwards into his face. Danson's colleague Graham Lee, I guessed, peering at transparencies on a light box. I wondered if any new images had arrived to add to Danson's distress.

From the desks on either side, I was being politely observed.

'Can I help you?'

If names reflect image I knew this must be Ginny. She was as languorous as a mannequin, had washed her tawny hair and walked out with it wet to be teased and fashioned by the breeze. I felt myself drowning in dark eyes set in a face no photographer would dare to retouch.

'Is Frank in?'

The man at the back of the room looked up.

'What's it about?'

His eyes were hard. After the discovery of the horrifying transparency I guessed they were all on pins.

'My name's Jack Scott. I'm doing some investigating for Frank.'

Danson had obviously kept him informed. He nodded, and said, 'Come on through. I'm Graham Lee. You've been talking to Ginny Felix. Claire Sim is the cute one doing all the work.'

He rose. I skirted Ginny's desk with a smile, glanced across and nodded to the room's third occupant and followed Lee through an interior door. He closed it behind us.

This room was the business's engine room, and looked lived in. Walls hung with charts and year planners, a couple of desks bearing banker's green lamps and computers and switched-off light boxes scattered with transparencies, two-tone filing cabinets in massed ranks, the aching string bends of a blues guitar solo curling like unseen smoke from hidden speakers.

It was mid-afternoon. In the hours since Calum and I had talked to Frank Danson he had rallied, reinforcing my own view that work and time can heal ills. When he swivelled to greet me his eyes were bright but questioning.

'I've been talking to a knowledgeable friend of mine,' I said as he nodded me towards a chair. 'His memory goes back a long way. What he told me contradicts your parting shots.'

'Remind me.'

'You said there were no suspects. That no relatives or close friends were investigated.'

'Ah. And your friend came up with Becky.'

'Bound to, wasn't he?'

I slid glossy photographic magazines onto the floor and dropped into the scruffy easy chair they'd hogged. Lee was at one of the desks, watching us.

'What I meant,' Danson said, 'was that those people questioned were released without charge.'

'But you didn't tell me Becky Long had been a suspect.'

'Why should I? I want you to find the kidnappers. To find out what's going on now, not waste time going over old ground.'

'After twenty years all the ground's old, Frank, but to me it's all new. Becky sounds like the ideal person to talk to. Ex-police. Jenny's sister, yet still a suspect. Suitably miffed at the time, she's bound to have followed up by asking her own questions of the right people. My friend is knowledgeable but an outsider. Becky will either know more, or see the same things from a different angle.'

Danson was thoughtful. 'If you say so. I don't think it'll help.'

I waited a moment. 'Does the name James Cagan ring a bell?'

He shook his head.

'Patricia Maguire?'

Same negative reaction.

I hesitated, knowing that the way forward was going to ruffle feathers.

'Yesterday you showed me a transparency that had been sent to this office. You said Ginny popped her head in to warn you. Did she see it arrive? Was she the first person to handle it?'

Danson's lips tightened. 'I told you, the envelope was missing.'

'That doesn't answer either of my questions.'

'I think Claire passed it to Ginny, then Ginny — '

'Passed what? Envelope or transparency?'

'When I went through, there was a transparency on the light box.'

'And it got here by magic?'

His face was frozen. The room was very quiet. I sighed.

'Frank, I'm trying to help you. Nobody's accusing your staff of any wrongdoing.'

Graham Lee cleared his throat.

'Claire has the keys and opens up,' he said. 'The mail's usually on the floor when she gets here. She's sorted it before the rest of us arrive.'

'And photographic material goes to Ginny?' He nodded.

'What about the envelopes?' I looked at Frank, then back to Graham Lee and shook my head. 'No, forget I asked that. I don't know why I'm bothering. If there was no identification on the mount, there'll certainly be no return address on the envelope.'

'And even if it was delivered by hand by the bastard who's doing this,' Frank Danson said, 'we'd be no wiser because it came too early.'

Or was brought in, I thought, by somebody who works here.

We were interrupted as Claire came through with three mugs of coffee. She was petite and light on her feet, perfumed for freshness not seduction but with short dark hair framing the face of a Mata Hari. Her dark eyes were guarded but wise. I guessed she was in her mid-forties, but she was one of those lucky people who will always look ten years younger than their age.

'At risk of treading on toes,' I said, as she slipped out and closed the door, 'I'd like you to tell me something about Ginny and Claire.'

'More time wasting,' Frank said.

'A woman was involved in the original crime. Ginny and Claire are both old enough — '

'Don't be bloody ridiculous. I trust them — '

'Tell me why.'

'Ginny's full-time, been here five years. Claire's worked here part-time ever since we opened. They've never put a foot wrong.'

'Their private lives?'

'Next of kin and so on, yes. Beyond that, it's none of my business.'

'But it could be mine.'

It was as if an iron door had clanged shut. I'd walked in on a rejuvenated man, demonstrated the merciless, prying qualities of a criminal investigation, and he didn't like it. Nevertheless . . .

'Humour me, Frank. Tell me if both Ginny and Claire were here, at work, between the 24th and the 30th of last month.'

He shook his head. 'Ginny was on holiday.'

'She went away?'

'I don't know what she did. She rang me on the Saturday — that *was* the 24th — and asked for the week off. She said it was urgent. But she didn't take a full week. She was back the next Saturday morning and worked the half day.'

'And Claire?'

'Claire was here, but I've already told you she's part-time.'

Graham Lee swivelled gently, his lips pursed as he thought back. Then he nodded.

'Claire was off quite a bit that week.' He rolled his eyes. 'I know I had more to do than usual, and she's still catching up.'

Danson grunted. 'So it was a week when both girls were away more than they were here. What's that done, cracked the case?'

'I wish!'

I thought of telling him of my vague suspicions about Cagan, but decided against it. As I placed my still-full coffee mug on the corner of his desk and stood up he turned away and scribbled irritably on a Post-it note. He stuck it on a card-backed manila envelope that was lying on his desk and handed it to me.

I had Becky Long's address and the ten by eight prints of the horrific transparencies.

In the sort of silence you might experience when someone has sworn in a cathedral, I showed myself out.

On my way I noticed that Ginny, standing up and smiling, was not as tall as I'd imagined. Medium height. Medium build. Medium everything.

I wondered if that was a clue.

9

Serendipity has always played a part in my investigations, and this one was no exception. The address handed to me by Frank Danson was on the other side of Woolton, a half-hour drive from town. I made it in less than that, drove through Woolton village in a stream of traffic and on the way out caught sight of a red-painted hut of corrugated iron. It was similar to a Baptist mission I'd known many years ago in Aigburth.

Bells rang. I peered hard across the tatty front garden at the peeling noticeboard with its fading Biblical quotations and exhortations, earned some road-rage honking from a following car as I veered dangerously, and drove on for another quarter-mile before I could back into a tight parking place.

If Frank Danson had estimated a time for my arrival at Becky Long's, and divulged it to the ex-policewoman in his phone call, she was going to be either disappointed or overjoyed. I would be late. The tin hut I had just spotted was almost certainly the mission run by Calvin Gay.

I walked back in the sunshine. The iron

gate squealed. Its rusting bars were rough against my palm. The path was cracked concrete where weeds flourished. Close up, the noticeboard was warped plywood split by wind and rain, the entrance a similarly neglected double door. I turned the tarnished brass knob and walked into a main room furnished with long benches set in rows before a six-foot trestle table that would be an altar at religious services, a desk at other meetings. My nostrils were assailed by dust, Pledge and another faint scent. Underfoot, floorboards squeaked like tired mice.

A tall man as gaunt as an old-fashioned coat-stand was watching me from a door leading to a back room. He had a white goatee and deep-set obsidian eyes.

'Calvin Gay?'

'Sure. And you're Jack Scott.'

A statement. The voice as soft as velvet, emerging from lips turning inwards like the slit punched by a chisel in a tin can. I did some mental backtracking and knew Danny Maguire had been talking to his boss, Gay had drawn the right conclusions when I walked in.

'Yes, I am. But this is an accidental encounter. I was on my way through and caught a glimpse of this place . . .'

'This place.' There was amusement in his

voice. 'I take it you were impressed?'

'Couldn't believe my luck.'

Gay grinned. 'Take a pew.'

I sat down. Gay joined me, sitting at the other end of a bench shiny with use.

'D'you find her?'

'Pat?' I frowned. 'Haven't you been told?'

His chest swelled as he took a deep breath. 'She's dead?'

I nodded.

'Damn!' He shook his head in disbelief. There was a lengthy silence as his mind grappled with the bad news. Then he seemed to shake himself.

'So that's it. They both left that morning — and now they're dead.'

'Were they close?'

'They worked for me but kept their personal lives to themselves; I don't know what they did in their spare time.' He looked at me, his sharp eyes interpreting my look. 'But, yes, they drove to Wales together, and now they're both dead. I'd say there was something connecting them, wouldn't you?'

'The connection I'm interested in may be different, and nothing to do with Bill Fox.'

He waited, let the silence build.

'Something has come to light that suggests a link between Pat and a crime committed twenty years ago.'

Still no comment. But a definite stirring, a flicker of interest.

'Does the name James Cagan mean anything to you?'

He nodded, the sharp eyes now on the alert. 'Sure. But James Cagan's also dead.'

'Was he someone Pat . . . visited, met . . . ?'

'One of our regulars. James was a petty criminal, a genuine weirdo. Over the years we've tried to help him. It's been a lost cause.' He shook his head. 'But not *twenty* years. No way. I know for certain Pat saw him for the first time when she visited him in gaol. That was five or six years ago.'

'You're sure of that?'

He thought about it, and shrugged. 'That's what I said. She came back from that first visit and told me she didn't know the man. Why would she lie?'

She'd lie, I thought, if she and Cagan had both, in some way, been involved in the Danson kidnapping. She'd lie if she'd withheld information from the police. I listened to the hum of traffic and suddenly pinned down that other scent as a trace of perfume on the air. At the same time I became aware of a keyboard clicking in the other room, the soft clearing of a feminine throat and thought at once of the women in Danson's office — medium build, medium everything — the as yet unidentified woman at Cagan's bedside.

'What about Frank Danson. Have you heard of *him*?'

'Ah. *That* crime. You're trying to establish a link between Pat Maguire's death and the kidnapping of those two kids.'

'The link's already there. I'm trying to work out what it means.'

I thought about what Gay had said, how readily he'd recalled the kidnapping. 'You were here then, weren't you? This mission was already up and running.'

'We opened in '75.'

'We?'

He smiled. 'Me. But I've had a lot of help since.'

And lost two assistants in a week, I thought. Well, I'd called at the mission on impulse, and so far what had I gained? I'd established that Pat Maguire knew Cagan well. If the warning Pat had received linked her to Danson and the kidnapping, then her knowing James Cagan meant that *his* involvement in that crime at the very least couldn't be ruled out.

'What do you remember about the kidnapping?'

Gay pursed his lips, frowning. 'The parents went out leaving a baby-sitter in charge.

When they returned early, the house was empty.'

'Suspects?'

He shook his head. 'None. The police found the baby-sitter. I think they talked to Danson's cousin.'

'Not Danson's. His *wife*'s — and it was her sister.'

He shrugged. 'Sister, cousin . . . '

I said, 'A photograph was left behind. It seemed to prove that two young men were involved. This was 1985.' I paused. 'I wonder where James Cagan was at that time.'

'Cagan was in prison,' Gay said.

'You said you didn't know him twenty years ago.'

Gay grinned and stood up. 'No, what I said was, we weren't *helping* him twenty years ago.'

'But you knew him?'

'From the outset, part of my vocation has been getting involved with prisoners.'

I accepted that, and recalled what he'd said earlier. 'What did you mean when you said he was a weirdo?'

'He was a loner. Few friends outside prison, nearly all of them male.'

'Gay?'

'Nope. James Cagan lived in the big wide world, but for as long as I knew him he'd placed himself in what amounted to voluntary, solitary confinement.'

* * *

Have you noticed how, when you change your car, every other car you see on the road becomes the same make. You buy a Ford, suddenly everyone's driving Fords.

Today, that's how it was with women. The ICU ward sister had told me the woman who sat watching James Cagan die was medium everything, and since then I'd not noticed a woman who couldn't comfortably slip into a size 12 dress. Is that medium? I don't know, but when the ward sister gave the description, that was the size that sprang to mind.

When she answered my ring Becky Long was dressed in jeans and a loose sweater. And she was medium. Even her hair was a snatched-back mid-brown. If I was about to treat every woman of average size as a suspect, I would soon be overwhelmed.

She led the way along a pleasant hall and into a sitting-room that was as comfortable as Frank Danson's was spartan. And she was a collector. I didn't try counting the lustrous, dove-grey porcelain figures, but no liqueur bottles would ever battle for standing room on a buffet that was, well, a monument to one person's obsession.

I was staring; she was watching.

'Introductions are a waste of time,' she said. 'I know you're Jack Scott, you know I'm Becky Long. So with that out of the way, sit down and tell me what you want.'

'Police efficiency,' I said, dumping myself on the settee. 'No beating about the bush, straight to the point.'

'You've come from Frank, so I don't need to ask how you know my background, or what this is about. But renewed interest after twenty years? Something's happened, hasn't it? Frank can't hide much from me. Few people can hide *anything* over the phone.'

She'd settled in a sumptuous chair. I noticed that medium went with the form, but not the decoration. Eye shadow had been applied unsparingly under arched black brows, and her lipstick was dark and glossy. She was Cleopatra in three-quarter trousers with Deva sandals revealing painted toenails; a not-so-ancient in modern dress; a contradiction with, I hoped, something to contribute.

As she made herself comfortable my eyes strayed elsewhere. It was a woman's room, no doubt of that, but I saw signs of a man's presence: casual shoes in the alcove alongside the chimney breast; a leather jacket on a hook behind the door.

Visitor, lodger? Or something much cosier because, according to Manny Yates, she was still unmarried.

I spent the next few minutes watching for reaction as I told her what I knew of the disturbing and baffling developments. She was familiar with the past and as Jenny's sister had grieved with Frank Danson, yet she registered little emotion as I told her about the new index card sent to Frank, the one sent to Pat Maguire before she fled, and the discovery of her body. I told her about Bill Fox's murder in those same woods, and the two transparencies Frank had received. I told her that the index cards, past and present, almost certainly established a link between Pat Maguire and the kidnapping. What I *couldn't* tell her was what I wanted, because I didn't *know* what I wanted.

'What I'm trying to do,' I said, 'is get people to open up in the hope of something emerging that gives me a lead. So far I've got the Pat Maguire connection, and a dead man called James Cagan whose corpse has been snatched.'

'Who's he?'

'I thought you might know.'

'Two men and a woman were involved in the kidnapping. The woman was seen by the baby-sitter, the men weren't. Are you saying

Cagan was one of them?'

'It's a possibility.'

'But this Pat Maguire was the baby-sitter?'

She saw my surprise.

'Come on,' she said, 'I'm an ex-police officer, and that one's easy-peasy. Tricia, short for Patricia. She was using her maiden name then, but so what? An index card popping through her letter-box on the same day Frank gets one. Twenty years after a kidnapping she let happen.'

'Let?'

'She let the bloody woman into my sister's house.'

'And that woman wasn't you?'

'I was elsewhere.'

'But not where you were supposed to be.'

She smiled enigmatically. 'Perhaps I was. But where I was supposed to be might not have matched where people *expected* me to be.'

'You didn't explain then, to the police — and you're not saying now?'

'No reason not to. It all happened a long time ago, didn't it?' She shrugged. 'When the kidnapping took place I was visiting a Manchester clinic.'

'What kind?'

'This is where I say, 'it's a woman thing', and you back off.'

I grinned. 'Woman things have become man things in the modern world. Nothing's sacred.'

'And the promotion issues I was facing at the time are no secret.' She smiled. 'I know you got that from Manny Yates — yes, the old fox has connections everywhere — so let's drop this line of thinking by saying that the visit to the clinic was entirely to do with internal police matters.'

I cocked an amused eyebrow. 'Internal?'

'Piss off.'

'And with possible connections to a certain senior police officer who — '

'Leave it!'

I took a deep breath.

Becky Long stood up.

'There's something else you haven't considered,' she said, watching me as I climbed to my feet and prepared to leave without scattering expensive ornaments. 'You're working on the theory that this Pat Maguire was the baby-sitter. And you've reached that conclusion because of an index card which you're assuming is a warning from kidnappers who are now up to some new wickedness.'

'Who else would send it?'

'Put that thought to one side for the moment, and consider this. Twenty years ago the police only had the baby-sitter's word that a woman impersonating me arrived at Jenny's house. Suppose that never happened. If you seriously consider that possibility, then Pat Maguire wasn't just a baby-sitter — she was one of the kidnappers.'

10

It was past nine and getting dark when I drove down to the banks of the Mersey and parked outside Calum Wick's Grassendale flat, climbed the stairs and let myself in. No lights, no human presence. As I dumped my jacket I realized I was hungry. I'd eaten breakfast early, watched Manny Yates indulge in a liquid lunch, abandoned an untouched mug of coffee in the back room of Danson Graphics and inhaled unwanted smoke in Becky Long's living-room.

It was long past dinner-time, but who likes eating alone?

Sian had left me at Manny's and taken a taxi to Allerton Road for her appointment with an estate agent. That would have taken an hour at the most. As she wasn't here I guessed she had gone on to the Calderstones' flat DS Meg Morgan shared with DS Joe Leary, and the spare room often used by Sian when she was in Liverpool.

Calum had gone to Renshaw Street to meet Stan Jones. Or maybe not.

I sat down in my usual leather chair, dug

out my mobile and dialled his number. No answer.

I tried Stan Jones. Stan was the white-haired scally whom I'd first met when he was suspected of all sorts of skulduggery in the Gerry Gault case. At that time he had a running argument with Gault — the knife thrower operating as Pedro and his Flashing Blades — about who had fathered the lovely Sadie Gault's child. It was only later that I learned of the scams he operated with Calum Wick that eventually led to their being accused of selling stolen cars and released for lack of evidence.

When Stan answered the phone his hoarse tones were just audible above background hubbub that could have been a full-scale riot at Night Owl or an unusually quiet night at the American Bar.

No, he hadn't seen Calum Wick.

I tossed my mobile onto the settee and let my eyes roam around the dim room where half-painted soldiers glittered in the half-light. Then, half-heartedly wondering if I should stir myself, I noticed the mail I must have walked over in my haste.

I went to the front door and gathered it, sat down, flicked Calum's mail after my phone and looked with interest at the one letter that remained.

94

It was addressed to me. And that *was* unusual. I spent a lot of time in Grassendale, but *all* my mail went to North Wales. This one had no stamp. It had been delivered by hand — and at once I thought of Frank Danson.

The contents of the square white envelope felt stiff. Like card.

A knot tightened in my stomach.

I inserted a finger. Ripped open the envelope. Extracted the contents.

It was a Get Well card. The cartoon picture was of a man in bed, thermometer in his mouth, his fat bandaged leg hoisted high by ropes and pulleys, one bandaged arm held stiffly at right angles. In a vase on the bedside table white lilies wilted.

The message on the front read: *Sorry to Hear You're in Hospital.*

On the inside page that was left blank for a personal message the sender had written, in letters fashioned with a now familiar red felt pen:

Watch your back, Scotty.

When heavy footsteps thumped on the stairs I was pacing restlessly with a mug of hot coffee in my hand. I had the door open before Mike Haggard and Willie Vine reached the landing, and I left it like that for them to troop through and close. They'd been here many times, but I was a little surprised that they'd agreed to come at my late call.

Detective Inspector Mike Haggard was big and burly in crumpled jacket and trousers. Smoke from the king-sized cigarette in his big fist did battle with the scent of Aramis aftershave. He glowered, dropped onto one end of the settee and looked pointedly at my still steaming mug.

Elegant and erudite, DS Willie Vine did his usual tour that took in Calum Wick's wall of fame and the work table where Light Dragoons awaited their coats of gloss enamel. He wandered around the coffee table, grinned at me and sat down in the spare chair.

'Ill Wind's down from the hills again an', as bloody usual, he's run out of puff,' Haggard said, using the name he'd tagged me with during the Gault case. 'So now he's going to soften us up with some of that instant swill he's drinkin', then pick our brains.'

'There's a cutting retort in there somewhere,' I said, making for the kitchen.

'Only cutting's not your forte,' Haggard called after me. His chuckle was hoarse. He'd dropped in a clever word for Vine's benefit, and was chuffed. I listened to the murmur of voices as they traded insults. When I carried two more steaming mugs through Haggard was still smugly smiling.

'If brains are there to be picked, I'll pick them,' I said, winking at Willie as I returned to my chair. 'But first, let me tell you a story.'

I began with Danny Maguire, moved to the corpse in the woods, skipping nothing en route from the hospital to Danson Graphics and my visit to Becky Long. I went into some detail so they got facts mixed with suspicion and supposition. On the way I got not a smidgen of reaction, but I sensed some interest in Willie Vine and knew that a policeman fond of books and statistics would have studied many past cases.

I finished with the Get Well card I'd received.

It was Haggard who spoke first.

'You're a PI. That means nosy bastard. Threats go with the job.'

'And must pertain to a current investigation.'

'Pertain!' He looked at Vine and shook his head in disbelief. 'A threat can pertain to whatever the perp wants it to pertain to.' He grinned savagely. 'Vine'll tell me I've ended with a preposition, but it still means you could be bein' threatened by someone else out of your murky past.'

'Red felt pen, the same as the other cards. Isn't that a clue?' I raised an eyebrow.

Haggard shrugged.

'So what d'you want from us? Nothing's been reported to the police by Danson, Maguire said bugger all to us until his wife turned up dead, your favourite Welsh DI and the North Wales police force started off handlin' the Fox killing and now with Pat Maguire they've got another. But if there's no crime here in Liverpool and a nasty letter doesn't warrant police protection — where do we come in?'

'There is a crime. It's very old, it's unsolved, and now it's been resurrected. I thought you should know, perhaps check through files — in your spare time.' I paused, thought for a moment and said, 'As I'm involved, I might be allowed a glimpse.'

Haggard puffed at his cigarette and shook his head in the swirl of smoke. 'It could be nothing more than someone wagglin' a big wooden spoon, couldn't it? Doin' some stirrin' because Danson's trod on their toes.'

'No. You're forgetting the transparency that brought this back to life. It shows the same two men as in the twenty-year-old colour print, taken at the same time because they're clearly holding Danson's boys, in his house.'

'What about the dead man, Fox, is he part of it?' Willie Vine said.

'I'm not sure. But I know he was in Wales with Pat Maguire. And the message sent to

Pat tells me she's definitely involved. She was probably the baby-sitter.'

'Or maybe not.' Haggard cocked an eyebrow. 'When you talked to Long she suggested the mysterious other woman could have been a red-herring. As in didn't exist. A phantom created by the so called baby-sitter to hide the fact that she herself was one of the kidnappers.'

'We'd already considered that possibility.'

'If Maguire was one of the kidnappers,' Willie Vine said, 'why did she get a card with a message?' He looked at me. 'What was it?'

'*Remember to forget*. Which suggests she knew too much.'

'Yeah, and it all adds up to your usual tangled bloody web of cryptic messages and clues plucked out of thin air,' Haggard said scathingly. 'Amateurs always delight in complications. They go rushin' around like headless chickens and suddenly everyone's a suspect.'

'Not everyone. Four women. Two of them work for Danson. One — Becky Long, the sister — was a suspect at the time of the kidnappings. And then there's Pat Maguire who, one way or another, is in it up to her neck.'

'*Was* in it,' Haggard said, and there was a brief silence.

'Assuming Pat Maguire was the baby-sitter,' Vine said, 'what about the two men?'

'I go with what I've got — '

'Or what you make up,' Haggard said.

' — and so far I've got just the one slender lead.'

Vine sipped his coffee. 'James Cagan?'

'Right.'

'Even slender's stretchin' it.' Haggard pulled a face. 'The only reason you're suspicious of him is because Pat Maguire, who *might've* been involved, also *might* have visited Cagan in hospital.'

'She certainly visited him in prison.'

'And you got that from a Yank with a mission.' Haggard grinned. 'So what about this Gay feller? Is he the second man alongside Cagan?'

I shook my head. 'Too old.'

'But there's something there you're not happy with?' Vine had been watching me closely. Erudite *and* astute. A formidable combination.

'He remembered the case too easily,' I said. 'And, through Pat Maguire, the mission *was* involved with James Cagan.'

Haggard was up out of his chair, wandering across to the window. He hooked the net curtain with a finger, lifted a corner and peered out.

'Accordin' to you,' he said, 'Pat Maguire was the baby-sitter when two kids were kidnapped, an' she's linked to Cagan through

100

this old Yank's mission.' Still holding the curtain, he turned to glare at me. 'Only, if we can believe what Calvin Gay told you, Cagan was in prison when the kids were snatched.'

Somehow he managed to pin me with a look that was both scornful and deferential.

'So while you're beating about ancient bushes, openin' cans of worms, and pluckin' suspects out of thin air, maybe you can do some real good. Help your favourite Welsh DI solve a couple of genuine current crimes. Like why Pat Maguire went missing for seven days, an' who killed her and Fox. Then do something for me: ask around your scruffy contacts, see if anyone can tell you who snatched Cagan's body from the hospital morgue, and why.'

I nodded. 'I'll be doing all of that while helping Frank Danson. I'll let you know if I come up with anything.'

But Haggard was no longer listening.

He'd turned back to the window. All of us heard the soft purr of a car engine, the slight squeak of brakes, doors slamming.

'Jesus Christ!' Haggard said, astonished. 'It's the fuckin' Gay Gordon — and he's got a woman with him.'

11

'Surprise surprise.'

Calum Wick grinned. 'Now why is that? Has Haggard's Gay Gordon sobriquet warped your perceptions? Did you think I was maybe buttering my toast on the other side?'

'Talking of toast,' I said, 'it's close to midnight. I haven't eaten since breakfast, so supper . . . '

'Let me.'

The voice was soft and warm, the form petite and shapely, the aura one to turn strong men's knees weak. When she walked into the room the mounted Light Dragoons seemed to sit more erect in their saddles, and I fought the urge to reach for a comb I rarely used. Dark hair framed her elfin face, but it was the huge eyes people would notice before surrendering without a whimper to drown in their mysterious, liquid depths.

She was watching me with amusement. On her hand as she fingered a drawstring on her thin fawn gilet a gold wedding ring gleamed.

I looked at Calum, a gangling moonstruck Scot fiddling with his beard as he watched her walk into the kitchen.

'Surprise surprise,' I said again, softly, and he lifted a hand and waggled it in caution.

'Her name's Georgie,' he said quietly. 'I met her in the Owl. We got talking and when I mentioned the yacht moored in Antibes that sort of swung it.' He grinned. 'Didn't it, Georgie?' he called over the clatter of dishes.

'Didn't what do what?'

'My charm. Sort of sneaked up on you and sandbagged you into submission.'

She poked her head out, frowning sweetly. 'Actually,' she said, 'it was the yacht what did it.'

Calum chuckled richly. He swung himself onto the settee, stretched out, kicked off his shoes and crossed his ankles.

'So, sleuth, what were Cassiday and Sundance doing here?'

'My invitation. They had to come in sooner or later, and ramifications in an already tangled web have led to personal threats against my body.'

I brought him up to date as coffee bubbled and the smell of hot toast and honey drifted through, and by the time the three of us were wiping butter off our chins and settling back with half empty mugs Calum had taken everything in and Georgie had, well, listened politely but without interest.

I couldn't have been more wrong.

'What you need to do,' she said, 'is talk to the girls at Danson Graphics.'

I blinked. 'Tell me more.'

'Think suspects and so on. You've spoken to Becky and Calvin Gay. Patricia Maguire's dead. Jimmy Cagan's body's been snatched. And you know Gina — '

'Ginny.'

'You know Ginny and Claire had time off on those important dates — and who else is close enough to Danson to know his every move?'

'Wow,' I said, and cast an awed glance at Calum. 'Have we got a vacancy for a super sleuth?'

'Consultant,' Georgie said.

'When can you start?'

'I just did. That'll be fifty pounds. A cheque's fine.'

'I'll notify my accountant,' I said. 'He's on Calum's yacht.'

'Damn,' Georgie said, and grinned at Calum as she stood up. 'I thought you said he was clueless?'

'Aye, he is, right enough — but where money's concerned, the word's tight.'

The banter was easy, the atmosphere unstrained. I got to my feet as Georgie made her way to the door. She stopped on the way at Calum's work table and placed her hands on its edges as she leaned forward to look closely at the half-painted figures.

'Not bad, but painters like Calum are two a penny,' I said. 'I'd sack him, but then he'd be forced to go back to Scotland and I wouldn't wish that on anyone.'

I fielded Calum's ferocious glare, heard him thank her for the lift home in her red Ford Ka, then returned her cheery wave as she left and was in the kitchen refilling two coffee mugs when the front door closed and he came through. He was wearing his usual leather jacket. On it, her perfume lingered. A month, and already so close . . .

Had I ever seen Calum Wick like this? No, never — and for the two of us that 'never' stretched back a good few years. And the thought came to me that in the midst of chaos there was order; while evil was creating one mystery, goodness was moving in that familiar, mysterious way. I knew I was waxing lyrical, but it pleased me immensely to see Calum Wick with a soul mate at a time when Sian and I were . . . well, moving close to co-habiting with intent — the intent, in both our minds, being to make it permanent.

'It's nothing, yet,' Calum said, pre-empting my question. 'We've been meeting most days at various odd times.'

'I knew something was up.' Then, unable to

resist, 'How does meeting you fit into her marriage?'

He shook his head in awe. 'Hawkeye, last of the Mohicans, never misses a trick!'

'Hmph. Except when it matters. Like on a case when it's life or death.'

'Her marriage is on the rocks, the man knocks her about,' he said, as we went through. 'I don't know what she does, or where she lives. I can't say I really care because, like I say, so far it's just — '

'Pleasurable dalliance?'

'Aye. Or maybe more than that.' He sat down. Sipped his drink. Mused for a while then sighed deeply.

'Talking of cases . . . '

'Yes, well, Georgie was spot on with her suggestion, but — '

'That was your next step anyway.' He nodded. 'Where else could you go? If we leave the hunt for the North Wales killer to our Welsh detective, you're left looking for somebody who's doing nothing worse than post nasty letters.'

He put his mug on the coffee table, picked up the card I'd left lying there and studied the sinister red lettering with his lips thrust out. Then he flicked it away.

'As you've had pointed out to you, the involvement of a woman came from the mouth of a suspect baby-sitter. If that woman doesn't exist, aren't you wasting your time talking to Danson's staff?'

'Elimination of a suspect is a step forward. And, until proved wrong, I've got to believe the baby-sitter's original statement and stick with my own theory.'

'Aye. Pat Maguire got a card. Therefore Pat Maguire was the baby-sitter. And we're hunting for that elusive woman who impersonated Becky Long.'

He was nodding slowly, off on another line of thought as we sat in silence.

'If we had a line on those two men in their pathetic black gear,' he said, 'there'd be something to get our teeth into.'

'Indeed. Relatives to question. The possibility of discovering who the men associated with. And maybe someone would come up with the name of a woman . . . ' I thought of the photographs Danson had given me, realized they were still in the car. 'Danson did those prints. I suppose I should have shown them to Haggard and Vine. But the men were masked in both pictures, with and without the kids.'

'Be worth a try. Small details often lead to positive identification.'

'In the morning. After Danson.'

My mind was back with Sian Laidlaw, my

Soldier Blue. I was convinced she'd decided to spend the night at Meg Morgan's. It was too late for her to come home, too late for me to phone. Or was it. I looked at Calum. He was sprawled out, dark eyes watching me, reading me like a book.

My mobile was on the table. He stretched, reached it with a bony hand and tossed it to me then rolled lithely off the settee and waved a hand as he went to his room.

She answered on the first ring.

'I drove by Calum's. Watched the sun on the river for a while.' She paused. 'Your car wasn't there.'

I nodded, basking in her voice.

'How was the estate agent? Did you find somewhere to live?'

'I don't know.'

'Mm. Now which way should I interpret that?'

'The very best way,' she said. 'As in, I don't know if.'

I could feel my heart thumping. 'Don't know if . . . what? Don't know if you *want* to find anything?'

'Mm.'

'So what are the alternatives?'

'I'm at Meg's.' She chuckled. 'Well, you've guessed that much. But that can only be temporary.'

'And you need somewhere permanent,' I said, 'at your age.'

'Sheltered accommodation.'

'With someone to look after you.'

'Will you do that?'

'Look for sheltered accommodation?'

She chuckled. 'Look after me, silly.'

'Always, and forever,' I said huskily.

She whispered something. I could almost feel her warm breath. I whispered back, switched off.

And so to bed.

12

Why did I go out again, that night?

For sentimental reasons — and because that's in the title of an old song to which you're sure to know the words, then you'll understand how I felt.

I remember I went out very late on a moonlit night during the hunt for Gerry Gault, driving all the way across Liverpool with too much of the Macallan in my blood then walking in the dank river air because I wanted to put myself close to where a man had died and, through perhaps imagined affinity, move closer to that difficult case's resolution.

So this latest nocturnal stroll could have been a natural reaction to Sian's telling me that she had driven to Grassendale that afternoon and, in my absence, spent a pleasant few minutes watching the sunlight glisten like spilled gold leaf on the rolling river. I was once again seeking affinity, this time putting myself close, not to a dead stranger, but to my Soldier Blue.

Because, if I recall it correctly, the first line of that old song said a lot about loving someone for sentimental reasons.

Without a word to the lanky Scot I suspected was already asleep I crept softly down the stairs and along the passage past Sammy Quade's dingy quarters and so out into the chill river air to stand on the grassy embankment looking out over flat water in which lights from the distant shore sparkled like reflected jewels and somewhere, very close, tidal waters lapped on slabs of black stone.

Then there was a flurry of movement. Sudden alarm was like a fist hitting the panic button that made alarm bells jangle.

And something very heavy and hard struck me a violent blow on the back of the head.

Pain sliced through my brain. Bones and muscles turned to water. I sank to my knees. There was a roaring in my ears, a tightness across my nose. I squeezed my eyes shut, saw dazzling flashes of light laced with angry red. With a strangled grunt I dropped forward, my hands flat on cold wet grass. I was on all fours, and helpless. My head was hanging, an intolerably heavy weight.

A boot slammed into my ribs. It drove the breath from my body, threw me off balance. A fist hooked out of the red haze, cracked against my cheekbone. I was driven backwards, legs doubled under me. A second swinging kick thudded into my upper arm; the wound that had been healing for a week ripped open. Another wild kick sent agony lancing through my thigh as I cupped both hands over my groin. I twisted, snapped my legs from under me, rolled desperately. But now I was face down, my arms drained of strength.

As they came at me I rolled again, over, over. Nausea welled. Stars and streetlights were lightning streaks against a red sky. Then someone swore. A door banged. A bellow of anger exploded through the night.

Head whirling, my face flattened against rank, moist earth, I listened to the thump of footsteps racing over the soft ground, the clatter as they hit tarmac and rapidly receded into the distance.

Day Three — Wednesday 12 October

The card they'd delivered was wrong. They didn't put me in hospital.

When Calum helped me back upstairs — it was he who had come roaring out of the flat with a towel girding his loins, a Highland warrior in a makeshift kilt putting Sassenach mercenaries to panic-stricken flight — and did a quick once over it was to discover a painful lump poking through the hair on the back of my head and my upper arm slick with blood that had leaked from the reopened gunshot wound. He'd tended to me with bandages and salve, slipped into jeans and sweatshirt, brought strong laced coffee through from the kitchen into a room where light from the Anglepoise created a snug haven within encircling shadows. It was a time and a place we'd been many times, the dead of night in a sleeping city, an old house creaking in the thick silence as we drank to our first success.

Success? Well, Calum was right, of course. Once again I'd poked a stick into a wasps' nest and evoked a furious response. My probing was threatening someone's plans — even if I didn't know what those were, or who was doing the planning and objected so fiercely to my prying.

Watching me nurse my hot mug of coffee as I mused, Calum was once again thinking ahead.

'If it's any consolation,' he said, 'this proves you've got them worried.'

'If I worry them any more,' I said, 'they'll die laughing.'

'Assuming you're not yet funny enough to kill them, isn't it about time we considered who them is — if you'll pardon my fractured

English. I mean, this them we're talking about sent two thugs along to point out the error of your ways with their shiny steel toecaps. Amateurs; pros would have used baseball bats. But they'll learn, and to avoid a repeat we need to do something pretty quickly.'

'Easy. Them is either somebody I've met and spoken to, or someone who's been watching me go a-calling.'

'Aye. So who was it you called on? Frank Danson, Becky Long, Danny Maguire . . . '

'Plus Calvin Gay, and three more who were present when I visited Danson at work. But you can forget Maguire. He doesn't go back far enough to know anything about mysterious notes or brutal kidnappings. And if his wife *was* the baby-sitter, she died in the woods below Llyn Elsi and the killer's moved on.'

Calum shook his head.

'That last bit's true, the first is pure nonsense.'

'Mm.' I nodded, seeing his point and my error. 'Maguire wasn't *married* to her twenty years ago, but that doesn't rule out his involvement in the Danson case — right? And who else knew *exactly* where she was going when she took Bill Fox to Betws-y-Coed and the bloody end of both their lives?'

'Well, Calvin Gay for one.'

'Yes. The man I called on by chance. The man who employed Pat Maguire and knew James Cagan.'

Then Calum voiced the very question I had already asked myself.

'We're floundering because the case we're looking into is twenty years old. Are we doing the right thing by starting in the present? Wouldn't we be more likely to get a lead by starting in the past?'

'Maybe not more likely — but certainly *as* likely,' I said. 'Trouble is, I've already decided the line between past and present is blurred. Danson and Becky Long were both there twenty years ago, but they couldn't — or wouldn't — help the police then so I can't see how they can help us now. What we *have* got is something that again blurs that dividing line: photographs from the past that have only just surfaced. It seems to me they're the only genuine link between past and present, the only genuinely new information, and I think we should look at them much more closely.'

'As you are somewhat infirm,' Calum said, 'I will trot downstairs and get them from your car while you refill the mugs.'

I tossed him my keys. He padded out. I limped into the kitchen and listened to him skipping nimbly down the stairs as close to me a black cat lazily rolled and purred and I poured coffee with muted groans of pain. Infirm was right: so slowly did I move that Calum was once again settled on the settee and watching with amusement as I lurched back in like a tanker in a choppy swell, hot coffee slopping over my fingers.

The manila envelope was unsealed. Calum slipped out the 10″ × 8″ prints, perched his wire specs on the end of his nose and squinted at the photographs through smeared glass.

'Clean them.'

'Hm?'

'We're looking for clues. You can't see.'

'If it's this Scotch mist that's bothering you, it was never a hindrance at Bannockburn.' He smirked, but took off the glasses, tugged his shirt out of his trousers and wiped the lenses. I regained my chair, sat down and watched with interest as he studied each picture in turn.

'The way we do this,' he said, eyes down, 'is I look at them, don't tell you what vital bit of information I've detected, then you do the same and we see if you're as clever as me.'

'And if you don't find anything?'

'Fat chance — but if I don't you get a rare chance to shine.'

I sipped coffee and sank into a position

116

that left me awkwardly twisted but was a comfort to my numerous wounds. After a while he leaned forward to place the first photograph on the table. He gazed at the second for almost a minute before emitting a grunt of satisfaction and discarding it with a quirky smile. The third was treated in the same way, but faster and without any reaction then sent to join the others on the table.

'Hm,' I said. 'That went according to this experienced PI's expectations.'

'Meaning?'

'We're trying to identify the two men. They're not in the third photograph, so that's ruled out. The first was taken in Danson's living-room before they went upstairs for the two boys: they're dressed from head to foot in black, their clothing is undisturbed. However, in the second photograph they've carried the boys downstairs and they're struggling to hold two spitting little wildcats. They're in a mess, their masks have slipped — '

'Not quite.'

'No, but you know what I mean. And I saw that smug grin so I know you saw something.'

'And now it's your turn.'

'Maybe I already know what's there.'

He peered at me over his glasses, black eyes glittering.

'If you do, isn't that what they call cheating?'

'It would be, but actually it was a team effort: watching you examine those prints made me realize what I'd *looked* at but not *seen*.'

'Aye, well what you and I have both noticed may be of little use,' Calum said. 'I take it we *are* referring to that wee tattoo?'

'Yes. It's half covered by a sleeve, but it looks like one of those hearts with a scroll underneath it.'

'In which a name is invariably written,' Calum said. 'So what do you propose? We wander through the streets of Liverpool asking male passers-by to roll up their right sleeve?'

'Show the photograph to Willie Vine.'

Calum nodded thoughtfully.

'The very man. If the photo's scanned there are computer programmes to enhance the tattoo so the name underneath it can be read. And through today's databases on the PNC, Vine will be able to identify known criminals by their distinguishing marks.' He grinned. 'Be nice for us if this guy's still active.'

'If he was here tonight,' I said, 'his activities — and intentions — were anything but nice.'

13

I headed for Danson Graphics immediately after a latish breakfast, leaving Calum bent under the Anglepoise painting Light Dragoons. The hours in bed had left me with some stiffness but remarkably little pain. I made it down the stairs without a stumble and, as I drove down town through rush-hour traffic I thought fleetingly of Sian's plans but, unlike my feelings of yesterday, I was without foreboding. She had walked away from the estate agent without buying a house or renting a flat. We had ended our talk with warm whispers of sheltered accommodation, and beneath the crags of Snowdonia I had a stone refuge an army couldn't breach. If I did have any concerns it was because the loss of her job left her out on a limb. The adventurous woman who had taught pale-skinned executives how to survive in the wild was suddenly without a future. I wasn't sure if being an assistant PI would fill that gap.

Once again I parked in the Paradise Street high-rise and walked up the gentle slope to Castle Street. The lights were on in Danson Graphics. With its familiar double ping the door admitted me to an empty front office. At the musical chimes Graham Lee poked his head out of the back room, saw me, and called me through.

When I walked in and shut the door Lee had gone back to his light box, transparencies, and a pile of brown envelopes. Danson was facing me, sitting back in his swivel chair as he swung restlessly to and fro. One of the brown envelopes was on his desk. From his face I could see he was torn by fierce emotions. I looked at him enquiringly.

'Where are your two young ladies?'

'Both off. My doing, I told them to take the day. Things are getting . . . fraught.'

'But business life goes on, surely?'

He shrugged. 'Gray and I can cope. And I need to talk things out without interruption.'

'Me, too. I was hoping to ask the girls some questions. Separately.'

Lee looked across. 'I talked to them. Ginny did go away, that week. She spent a few days in North Wales. Claire's mother was in hospital so she was visiting her twice a day.'

I digested the information and felt a surge of anger. 'You should have left it to me.'

'Why? I asked in an off-hand way, they answered without hesitation.'

'And now they're both on their guard.'

'I told you I trust them.' Danson had

surged angrily out of his chair, and now he leaned across, grabbed the brown envelope and flipped it to me. 'For God's sake, forget the girls. Sit down. Look at that, tell me what you think.'

I sank into the worn chair, opened the envelope and slid out another photograph. Once again it was a 5″ × 5″ colour print, two young men gazing woodenly at the camera. No masks, no black clothing. Possibly not the same two men and, as the thought crossed my mind, I knew at once what Frank Danson was thinking, why he was in turmoil.

It was a medium close-up. Both men were dressed in white T-shirts, both were fair haired — as were the two young children featured in photographs two and three. Probably twenty years old — which was pushing Danson's hopes sky high. But it was a strange picture. My first thought had been that the subjects were looking at the camera with the blank gaze one associates with police officers and criminals. The thousand-yard stare. Their eyes *did* appear blank, but a closer look told me that what I was seeing was not the blank gaze of the hardened criminal but a deliberate attempt by two young men to mask their feelings.

And the feeling I was sensing was a terrible fear.

'Well?'

Danson, sitting down again, foot jiggling impatiently, eyes hot and searching.

'When did this come?'

'Last night. To the house.' His grin was fierce. 'Only this time I was quicker. I heard the letter box and charged through. When I opened the front door I saw the bastard running down the drive. A man, tall, not young. He looked back and laughed. And then he was gone, like the clappers, into a car that shot away as soon as he got in. I got close enough to put a dent in the boot with my fist.' He shrugged.

'The car's make?'

'Didn't notice.'

'So if it sped away, there were two of them.'

He nodded.

'What about the driver? Man, woman?'

'I don't know. Dark hair. Not very big.'

I was still holding the photograph. He looked at it, lifted his eyes to my face.

'What do you think?'

'I'm sorry.' I pulled a regretful face, shook my head. 'These men are not your boys.'

He made a fierce, angry exclamation.

'You can't be sure.'

'I'm positive.'

'Right age, same colouring, same hair — '

'No. It's not them.'

His voice was ragged. 'For Christ's sake, it follows the pattern. Think of the photographs. First it was the two kidnappers. Then the kidnappers holding the boys. Then the same boys a little older. Now this, twenty year olds . . . '

'I'm going to Admiral Street police station. I'll take all the photographs with me and ask questions.'

'You can ask till the cows come home. My boys are alive, and you're holding the proof.'

He could not be dissuaded. I didn't try again. Instead, I stood up, looked across at Lee.

'Could you let me have the girls' addresses?'

His lips tightened, but he scribbled on an index card and handed it to me.

'You're wasting your time,' Danson said.

'A man and a woman were murdered in North Wales. A criminal died in hospital and his body was snatched. Ginny and Claire chose that week to take time off. And where did they go?'

I left the question hanging and walked out as they thought about it in a thick, suffocating silence.

★ ★ ★

'So why isn't it them?'

DI Haggard was behind his desk in shirt sleeves, tie hanging loose under the white

123

shirt's open top button, thick dark hair as straggly as a bird's nest in winter. He was holding the latest photograph in one big hand. In the other a king-sized cigarette smouldered.

'Look at this one.'

I passed him photograph number two, the one in which two masked men struggled to hold Danson's screaming, kicking children.

He studied it and without a word passed both photographs to DS Willie Vine.

'What d'you reckon?'

Vine glanced only briefly.

'Same men.'

'Them holdin' the boys, those two in T-shirts?' He noted Vine's swift nod, and said, 'And you're basin' that opinion on the tattoo?'

'I'll get both pictures scanned, the tattoo enhanced.' Vine shrugged. 'But there's really no doubt.' He looked at me. 'Right?'

'I told Danson they were not his boys, but not my reason for being so sure.'

'Let me guess,' Haggard said. 'You're playin' cagey, cards close to your chest.'

'Until I know who's doing what to whom.'

'To whom,' Haggard said, and grinned at Vine.

'Enhancing that tattoo,' I said, 'should give us the name of at least one of the kidnappers.

I can't imagine why this wasn't picked up at the time of the kidnapping.'

'Remind us,' Haggard said. 'When exactly was that?'

'Eighty-five.'

'Before the Police National Computer,' Haggard said.

'Nevertheless . . . '

'Even before me an' Willie.' His savage grin left his eyes bereft.

'But now we're here,' Vine said, 'the computer's been on line for donkey's and within minutes all will be revealed.'

Since my last visit their office had taken on a new look and I knew from the changes that it was now their permanent home. Drab walls had been painted green, two more desks had been brought in and a computer with a coloured ball like a psychedelic goldfish floating across its screen sat on one of them alongside a printer big enough to eat into the world's precious forests.

That was where Vine was sitting, half turned to face us.

The computer was there for him to use, through it he could access vast amounts of information, but he had photographs to scan and enhance and for that he needed more equipment. He pushed his chair back, nodded at Haggard and walked out of the room leaving me alone with the grizzly DI with whom I had a relationship teetering precariously between respect, rivalry and reluctant admiration, the whole soured by the distrust of the professional policeman for the ex-army amateur who dabbled in crime when he wasn't making toy soldiers.

Haggard was still brooding over the other two photographs, his gaze dark. He discarded the one that twenty years ago had been left at the scene of the crime, looked more closely at the two youngsters playing in the gardens of the big house, then sat back. He flicked the picture thoughtfully with a finger.

'Where's this?'

I shrugged.

'Come on! Pound to a penny it's your home turf.'

This time I stirred, suddenly interested.

'Why?'

'Dry-stone walls. Mountains. All right, could be Scotland, the Lake District — even Derbyshire, at a push. But if I was a bettin' man . . . '

'A few years after the kidnapping makes it at least fifteen years ago. Ten to one the people have moved, so even if we do locate the house, what does that give us?'

'It's worth a try. Accordin' to this photograph those kids lived there, in that house — or maybe they were visitin' — '

'Or they were posed in the garden when the owners were out and someone wanted deliberately to lay a false trail.'

'Yeah, and I've told you, amateurs love complications. Fuck me gently, why would anyone go to all that trouble five years after they'd got away with a well-planned kidnappin'?'

'Hold on, just think of the photograph and card Danson got at the time. *Wait, Frankie, wait.* The next, with more photographs, after a gap of twenty years: *The waiting is over.* That suggests a long-term plan, doesn't it? They're visibly active now — whoever *they* are — and going to a *lot* of trouble. But I'm coming to the conclusion that they've *never* been completely dormant. Something's been going on behind the scenes for all that time, and we don't know what, or why Danson was targeted — why, suddenly, he's being persecuted and people are dying.'

The door clicked open, swung wide enough to bump the wall and Willie Vine came back in. He sat down, leaned across to place the photographs with the other two on Haggard's desk.

'The investigation into the kidnapping of the Danson kids was thorough,' he said. 'Evidence was gathered meticulously, but there were no leads and every line of enquiry led to a dead end. Until a week later, when the bodies of two young men were found on waste ground in Wavertree. They'd been murdered, executed by a single shot to the head. Neither had previous convictions, their prints weren't on record — '

'But one of them,' I said, 'had a tattoo on his right arm.'

Vine nodded. 'But no name in the scroll.'

'Damn.'

'It's interestin', though,' Haggard said. 'I mean, if those fellers in black fancy dress ended up dead, who was the killer?' He looked at Vine. 'They were positively linked to the kidnappin', but the killer was never found, right?'

Vine shook his head. 'No. They weren't linked. There was suspicion, but the tattoo meant nothing because this photograph' — he pointed to photograph number three — 'has only just been brought in by Ill Wind.'

'And according to all the evidence uncovered at the time, that leaves only one suspect — the woman who was let into Danson's house by the baby-sitter,' I said.

Haggard shook his head. 'Nah. Can't see it. Maybe she masterminded the kidnappin', but all on her own there's no way she could've made those two fellers stand still while she took a snapshot then put a bullet in their heads.'

'So there's always been a third man there behind the scenes?' I cocked an eyebrow.

'Man or men,' Willie Vine said. 'Two snatching the boys, plus another. And before you jump, let me tell you I've checked up on James Cagan, and he *was* in prison at that time in 1985.'

'So we can rule him out.'

'I told you before, he was never in,' Haggard said. 'Accordin' to you he *might've* been involved because Pat Maguire *might've* visited him in the Royal — only none of that happened, it was speculation gone mad.'

'All right.' I spread my hands, dropped them heavily onto my thighs. 'Cagan's out of it, the kidnappers have been dead twenty years and if the mysterious woman didn't murder them then someone else is out there.' I hesitated. 'That latest photograph was delivered by hand. Danson was quick enough to catch sight of the deliverer. A man. Not young. And there was a car waiting to whip him away.'

'Brilliant,' Haggard said with a glare.

'He's talking to me, and I'm talking to you, passing everything on.'

'Which makes it too fuckin' late for us to be of use.'

'He's got a long memory: you were no use twenty years ago.'

Haggard's lips tightened. The cigarette was doing nothing but spill ash. He mashed it in an ashtray, climbed out of his chair. I did the same, in the manner of a very old man. Haggard noticed and waited, his hands flat on the desk.

I forced a shrug. 'The warning card was followed up. I'm bruised but unbowed — and not in hospital.'

He growled something unintelligible.

Willie Vine handed me the photographs.

I walked out to my car clutching them, knowing they were clues that had already led to two dead men and wondering with trepidation if photograph number three was the last Frank Danson would ever see of his two sons.

And even at that point, with harbingers of doom gathering in the wings as the corpses piled up, I sensed that whoever was out there was going to far too much trouble just to show a bereaved man two dead bodies.

14

I walked down the hill, ordered an excellent latte in a Whitechapel coffee bar, drank it without haste then crossed the road to Paradise Street for the Quatro. The drive out of the city was through a fine, grey drizzle that inevitably reminded me of the afternoon I had climbed through the woods with Danny Maguire to where lightning flashed and cold rain beaded a dead man's face. Yet after almost three days I still couldn't be certain if Bill Fox's murder, or the one discovered soon afterwards, were linked to the Danson case.

Although small-time crook James Cagan being eliminated sent my investigation reeling backwards like a drunk who'd walked into a lamp post, I still had several possibles for the man both Vine and Haggard knew must be out there. Danny Maguire was only an outside bet; he had contacted *me* when his wife of eight years went missing. Calvin Gay, on the other hand, was another man close to Pat Maguire — who was almost certainly the gullible (or treacherous) baby-sitter — and his contacts with prisoners meant he would certainly know more than one man willing to kill for the right price.

Of the people I'd met so far, that left Graham Lee — Gray to his friends. Yes, I was forced to consider Danson's closest colleague, because if members of the family were always the first suspects in a murder investigation, close friends were never far behind.

But of course, if my instincts were right then I wasn't investigating a murder. Not yet, anyway.

The first address Lee had scribbled on the card was in Penny Lane, a location indelibly etched in my mind as the home of Oliver Dakin, the loopy vet in the Gault case. Ginny Felix lived higher up, closer to Smithdown Place, and I could hear the dull rumble of heavy traffic on Smithdown Road as I pulled into the kerb and stepped out of the car.

I hadn't phoned ahead. If she was out, I was wasting time. If she was in, surprise gave me the advantage. I knocked, waited, heard soft footsteps and stepped back. When the door opened, tawny-haired Ginny was looking at me with innocent dark eyes. If she was surprised it didn't show, and I found myself wondering if Graham Lee had cut me off at the pass by phoning ahead.

'Hello.'

She smiled.

'Did Gray telephone to tell you I was coming?'

'I don't know. The answering machine's flashing, but I've just come in. Would you . . . ?' She gestured vaguely.

'If you've got a minute.'

I followed her into a cosy hallway and shut the door. We went past the dark stairs into a living-room overlooking a back yard she had turned into a delightful patio where trellised flowers bloomed. A short coat had been thrown over a chair, shoes dumped on the mat in front of the hearth where a modern gas fire hissed and glowed.

On the table a cafetière with it's plunger unplunged stood alongside a lone china cup and saucer. Ginny smiled at me, left me to inhale the aroma of hot coffee like a nicotine addict doing some passive smoking and returned with a second cup. She poured. I sat down. She handed me a cup.

'So,' she said, curling into her chair like a fawn, 'what's this all about?'

'Background.' I gave a reassuring smile. 'Frank tells me what he thinks I should know. To help him, I need to find out from others what he might be leaving out.'

'Accidentally.'

'Of course.'

'So, fire away.'

I sipped coffee to marshal my thoughts, felt myself drowning in those wide dark eyes and asked the first question to pop into my head.

'How long have you been with him?'

'Professionally?'

'Well . . . yes.'

She smiled. 'It's all right. I thought you might be thinking . . . you know.'

'If I was, you've answered me — I think. But what about the job? How long have you had it?'

'Five years.'

'And you knew Frank before that?'

'I knew the story. About the kidnapping. The job interview was the first time we'd met.'

'How'd that happen?'

'Advert in the *Echo*. I phoned, he called me in and recognized my talents.'

'Photography?'

She pursed her lips and rocked her head from side to side.

'Mm, not really, not in the sense of taking pics. More like an eye for a good photograph taken by somebody else. So I could be a first-line filter removing the genuine crap.'

'Like you were the other day when that transparency arrived. The one with the two men holding his sons.'

'Oh, God, yes! But a fat lot of good I was. I

gave the game away by poking my head in for Gray. Really, I should have dumped it.'

'And you've no idea how it arrived?'

'Claire does that. Gathers the mail when she opens up.'

There was a moment's silence while we sipped coffee. I was going over old ground and getting nowhere. Was it time to be blunt?

'You were off work for a week recently. Where did you go?'

She was holding the saucer on steepled fingers, steadying the cup with her other hand. She said, 'I thought this was background. All about Frank Danson and Danson Graphics.'

'I spread my nets wide.'

She chuckled, and it was like thin ice crackling.

'I went to North Wales.'

'Where?'

'Here and there.'

'Specifically.'

She shook her head. 'No. It can't possibly help, and it's none of your business.'

'For as long as it takes, Frank's business is my business, and as you work for Frank . . . '

She shrugged. 'No, sorry. But that's it.'

Flatly. No argument.

I burnt my lips trying to finish the coffee as I stood up, almost cracked fine china putting

135

the cup down. Ginny was hiding something and she knew I knew it, but pushing would get me nowhere. I let her follow me to the door, opened it, stepped out ducking my head against the grey drizzle.

'I know you're helping Frank,' she said, 'but I really don't understand why you're questioning me.'

'You said you knew the story.'

'I know his kids were taken, and never found.'

'There was a woman involved,' I said. 'She'd be your age now.'

'Jesus! And you think — '

'I start close to home and work outwards.' I smiled. 'It's routine, and sometimes gets results — and they don't come much closer to Frank than you and Claire Sim.'

★　★　★

Win some, lose some.

Claire Sim lived in a flat on the second floor of a block on Ullet Road overlooking Sefton Park. All the doors were painted different primary colours. She was out. The man in the next flat heard me hammering on the door and came charging out. Against his yellow door he was as grey as wet newspaper and looked as if he'd spent the morning with his fingers in an electric socket.

'Give your fuckin' fist a rest and try the club.'

'I haven't got a club.'

He sneered. 'The club off Lark Lane, dickhead. Kingman's.'

'Not the KING OF CLUBS?'

'He 'asn't gorranother — has 'e?'

I grinned. 'I'll try it — and thanks.'

What goes around comes around.

It was a morning for clichés. Cut off at the pass, win some lose some, goes around comes around. And I was still smiling when I climbed into the Quatro and pointed it towards Lark Lane because the first time I entered George Kingman's sleazy club had been at the start of the Gault case and I'd been going back there ever since.

It was pushing lunchtime and there was a certain buzz in guessing who I'd meet there. Calum himself was wont to call in, as was DS Willie Vine, and Stan Jones of the rusty white van and thin grey beard would often be seen padding across the big room slopping the latest drink and trailing Old Holborn fumes and complaints.

The club was in Pelham Grove, two tatty terraced houses united under a lurid red neon crown. When I pushed through the greasy curtain that served as a door, slapped down the brown-linoleumed passage and turned into the main room, it was almost empty. Claire Sim was sitting on a high stool at the flashy bar looking moodily across at the deserted wooden platform where a forlorn microphone drooped. George Kingman was perched behind the bar reading the *Sun*. Heavy gold glinted at his wrists; sovereign rings on his fingers were heavy enough to put muscles in his forearms and under the harsh strip lighting sweaty skin glistened through his grade one haircut.

I came up behind Claire and touched her on the shoulder. She started. George Kingman looked across and rolled his eyes.

'The private dick. How's it goin', Shamus?'

'As well as,' I said. 'Give me something that's not Vat 69 and comes in your clean glass, George.'

This was a standing joke dating back to the first time we'd talked in his upstairs room when the only light was the blood-red glow from the exterior crown, the only drink Vat 69 diluted with ditch water, and below us in this very room a vet was rehearsing a Sinatra impression that ended up as a killer's swan song.

Claire had turned to face me and was watching with cool blue eyes. I climbed onto the next stool as Kingman poured whisky and slid the glass across the bar.

'I like your next-door neighbour,' I said, and, as she pulled a face, I noticed that her short dark hair was streaked with grey and thought of the ward sister's description. Excitement stirred. I wondered how I should play this. Or if, as was likely, I was again flogging a dead horse.

She caught my sudden look of interest.

'What?'

'How's your mother?'

'Still poorly.'

Kingman's paper drooped. His head half turned and I knew he was listening.

'I am sorry. Will she be in hospital long?'

'Hard to say.'

'Graham Lee said you've been visiting her every day.'

'Most days.'

She stopped then because Kingman had turned, caught her eye and nodded towards the entrance. When I looked to my right I saw a man all the way across the room. He was waiting in the shadows and I got the impression of hard features and cold eyes. Then Claire was down off the stool and had clip-clopped across the room to join the man I guessed had come to take her home, a woman with dark hair going grey who was yet another of those who would have either an M or a 12 on a label inside her clothes.

I tasted the drink, pulled a sour face and slipped from the stool. How do you get a picture to show a witness when the subject's just walked away? Why would I want to anyway? Wasn't James Cagan a closed book? Maybe — but for some reason I kept coming back to him. Gut instinct. The stubborn refusal to let a well-reasoned theory be discredited.

So, what about that picture I needed? Well, if the person you want checked frequents a certain club which has a board on the wall alongside the bar where a hundred photographs of drunken clients are stuck with pins or Blue-tack — you just might be in luck.

I took two steps to the side and examined the grubby cork board, looked at photographs of laughing couples with glossy permed and gelled heads rubbing together at tables where bottles and glasses glittered, groups of dancers draped in each other's arms as they tried to stand still for the camera; looked, looked again, and found in a cluster of Karaoke shots a photograph of Claire Sim on the platform, under the spotlights, mike in hand. Recent. Instantly recognizable.

'Can I have this?'

'What for?' Kingman had come around the bar and was looking over my shoulder.

'I'm a Helen Shapiro fan,' I said earnestly, as I peeled the photograph off the board.

'You've got a bump on your head. It's affected your brain.'

'That, or the VAT 69.'

He'd put the same drink in a different glass. I'd twigged. He was nonplussed. I walked away in the silence. He called after me.

'Listen. If Claire's visitin' Marg every day, she's doin' a lot of fuckin' mileage.'

'Ullet Road to the Royal. How far's that?'

'Try Ullet Road to the Costa.'

I'd been drinking whisky, but the tingle was not from strong spirit.

'Spain?'

'Her ma's Margie Sim. She's been out there a month. Visitin' her exiled husband.' He grinned and winked. 'An' there's proof, if you want it. Remember Solly?'

'How could I forget.'

'Yeah, well, Solly was in one of them fuckin' big holiday tenements on the coast, same resort. He came back yesterday. Margie's still there, for certain, 'cause our Solly was knockin' back the vino with her every night of his stay — so if Claire's been visitin' Marg every day she's clockin' up enough air miles to buy herself a return flight to Wagga Wagga.'

15

I drove straight down town, pulled into the Royal's car park and made my way through the hospital to the ICU. When I approached the desk a different nurse was chewing her lip as she concentrated on what looked like the same paperwork. She looked up as I approached.

'I called in yesterday,' I said, 'and spoke to a ward sister. Fair hair, blue eyes. D'you know if she's here?'

The nurse shook her head. 'That's Chris. It's her day off.'

'Ah.' I hesitated. 'Are you on this ward permanently?'

'More or less.'

'So you'd have been on duty at some time when James Cagan was here?'

Suddenly the look was guarded. 'Why?'

'It's all right, I'm not interested in the dead man, or where he's gone — or been taken. But I think I might know the woman who was visiting him, and I was wondering . . . '

I took out the photograph from the KING OF CLUBS, and passed it to her. She took one swift look, and nodded.

'Yes. That's her. In the week before Cagan died, she came in every day.'

⋆ ⋆ ⋆

From the car-park where the rain was now drumming steadily on the roof of the Quatro, I phoned Alun Morgan in Wales.

Why? Well, when I was in Australia there was a television personality called John Laws who advertised insect repellent and who would close the sequence by saying, 'When you're onto a good thing, stick to it.'

So what the hell's that got to do with a telephone call to Wales, you ask me? Yes, all right, so it does sound like the kind of rambling explanation you might get from a yachtsman who spends his sailing life on the wrong tack — but the point is when I left Haggard and Vine I had nothing, the kidnappers were dead, the baby-sitter was dead and a man who might not have any connection to the case anyway was not only dead, but missing. Yet now, out of nowhere, I found myself presented with two possible, red-hot leads. One had just been confirmed by the nurse — more or less; the second needed chasing and, once again, I was being pushed by gut instinct.

The Welsh DI answered at once, and

having read my caller ID, he jumped the gun.

'D'you find him?' he said.

'Who, Cagan?'

'Well now, I know you're a careless bugger, but just how many *have* you lost?'

'None, so far — which for me is surprising, I know — and you know damn well it wasn't me who lost Cagan. Anyway, I want to talk to you about Bill Fox and Pat Maguire.'

'Still dead, both of them.'

'Ah, but have you got any leads? Have the Welsh bloodhounds picked up the scent? Is the sound of furious baying echoing through the valleys?'

'Kind of you to ask,' he said, 'but I thought it was you supposed to be helping me?'

'Mm. You've been talking to Haggard. I wondered why you enquired about Cagan. But I didn't ask my question out of kindness. I need to know.'

'Point taken, and who am I to refuse the famous PI?' he said. 'No, there are no promising leads, but we're trying to trace a person who might be able to help us with our enquiries.'

'Yes?'

'A woman.'

'Go on.'

'Medium height and build, hair described as a sort of golden colour.'

'Tawny.'

'Seen wandering through the woods near Llyn Elsi the day before the bodies of Fox and Maguire were discovered.'

'What time were they murdered?'

'Fox had been dead twelve hours or so when you saw him. Maguire about the same.'

'And this woman?'

'Acting suspicious. Whatever that means, and you can be bloody sure I'll find out. Might have been carrying a camera.' He paused, ominously. 'What d'you mean, tawny, Jack?'

'A sort of golden colour.'

'Yes, and bollocks to you, too,' he said. 'But if I find out you know something and you're withholding information — '

'Sorry Alun,' I said, 'the signal's breaking up.'

I switched off and slid down in my seat with a smug grin.

★   ★   ★

The Ginny Felix lead looked promising — though where it was going was anybody's guess — but before driving out of the car-park I tried to analyse my obsession with James Cagan.

His name had first come to me from Alun

Morgan. According to Sian at the time, the Welsh DI had been feeding me the information in the hope that I'd draw the obvious conclusion: Cagan died around the time the cards began arriving and Pat Maguire went missing, so there had to be a connection. As I had, only minutes before Morgan's phone call, decided that Pat Maguire had been the Dansons' baby-sitter — and in all likelihood had visited Cagan in hospital — it had seemed logical that cards, timing and Pat Maguire could be brought together to connect Cagan to the kidnapping.

Only from Willie Vine I had confirmation that James Cagan had been in prison at the time.

End of story.

Except I now had convincing evidence that Claire Sim, who had worked for Danson ever since he set up in business, was the mysterious woman who had visited James Cagan in hospital.

A connection of some kind was restored. There was a lot to be unravelled, and the unravelling could result in a completely innocent explanation — but an unreasonable obsession was beginning to look more and more like a hunch that could pay off.

The knowledge gave me a warm glow. I had no hip flask nor the need of one for, wrapped in self-satisfaction inside my expensive personal cocoon on which the rain drummed hypnotically, I leaned my head sideways against the window and drifted into a dreamless sleep.

★ ★ ★

'So, you went to sleep?'

'For an hour.'

'Because you were chuffed?'

'A dead case came alive. A frustrated PI looking at a blank wall pursued his investigations, saw a window in which faint light gleamed, and hopped through.'

It was pushing six o'clock and we were in the kitchen eating cold pepperoni pizza with sliced tomatoes and crisp red onions washed down with half a bottle of warm stale Hock.

Satan was prowling like a black panther, preferring pizza to the expensive cat food he was snootily allowing to congeal in his dish. Calum was showered and changed, no sign left of the man who, when I walked in, looked as if he'd spent the day doing a Jackson Pollock on the floor with spilled Humbrol enamels. He had, of course, been applying the finishing touches to four more of the Light Dragoons, and while paint adhered to Calum where it spattered — beard, glasses, and most of his clothes — I knew that when I examined the miniature soldiers each button and ribbon would be crisp and clear, no drooping moustaches would be adrift on thin upper lips, no tiny eyes would be permanently crossed.

I'd walked in an hour ago, watched Calum painting with his tongue in the corner of his mouth as I filled him in on the latest developments, then wandered into the kitchen to drink a Macallan on ice and do something about a meal.

Now, the meal that had been consumed in the heavy silence of deep thought was almost finished. Calum pushed his plate away and went to the work top to spoon coffee into the percolator. I crunched manfully through the last burnt pizza crust, reached for the wine to wash away what tasted like dried-out charcoal and sat back aware of a growing realization that hot leads often finish up as cold cases. With the Danson kidnapping, Merseyside police came to that conclusion twenty years ago.

But we were cleverer than them — weren't we?

I put it to Calum. He placed the percolator on the stove and turned with folded arms to lean against the work top and look at me over his glasses.

'Let's say we're cleverer than most if we've got something genuinely of use.'

'And you don't think we've got much with Ginny and Claire?'

'People act furtively for any number of reasons. Those two girls became tight-lipped when a nosy PI started asking questions — and who wouldn't.'

'I said nothing to Claire other than to ask after her mother's health. Which told me she was lying, not only to me but to everyone at Danson Graphics. But isn't it our business to be nosy? And it surely can't be coincidence, Ginny being in the woods where murder was committed, Claire visiting Cagan every afternoon for a week?'

'Aye, and now we're back to wee Jimmy, the mysterious Mr Cagan who's done nothing of note but is currently top of your list — for something or other that hasn't yet been specified. He was not one of the kidnappers, and there's no way he could have been behind — or even part of — this latest sinister campaign.' He whipped off his glasses, jabbed one of the arms in my direction. 'Also, you're supposed to be hunting one woman and suddenly you're crowing over two suspects. You're dreaming up a case against both of them, but surely one's got to be eliminated, or we'll end up

149

with a whole bloody army of kidnappers.'

I pushed away from the table, went through into the living-room and clicked on the table light. Calum came through with two steaming mugs and sprawled on the settee, legs up, ankles crossed. We sat there in what, for several minutes, was a contemplative silence.

There seemed to be a lot of those, which suggested we were perplexed, but resolute.

The comfortable quiet was broken when Satan came padding through, saw Sian wasn't there and leaped onto the settee to curl up, purring, at Calum's feet. His yellow eyes widened as a gust of wind sent rain pattering on the window. In the downstairs flat there was a thud that could have been Sammy Quade falling out of bed.

'If there is a sinister campaign being waged against Frank Danson,' I said, 'we need to know its aims.'

'If we knew that,' Calum said, 'we might see a pattern and be able to work out what's likely to happen next. Or leapfrog over the next wasteful stages and catch the bandits with their pants down.'

'Mm. Haggard would like that plural: he's convinced there's a man or men helping the woman.'

'Your enviable assortment of bruises,' Calum said, 'testifies to that.'

'All right, so whoever is behind it has given Danson a picture of the kidnappers, waited twenty years then shown him the kidnappers with his sons, then children he believes are his sons playing in an unknown garden, and finally the kidnappers prior to their murder.'

Idly Calum scratched Satan's scarred ears, watched the black moggy stretch all four limbs and relax languidly into a prodigious yawn.

'So where is all this leading? And what can he expect next? More photographs? The end game?'

'We'll have to wait and see.'

I looked deep into the steaming coffee mug for inspiration, absently listened to a car door slam, footsteps on the pavement — then on the stairs.

They stopped. There was a soft tap on the door.

I looked at Calum.

'But perhaps not for too long,' I added.

Calum pushed away the surprised, meowing moggy, swung his feet down and crossed to the door. When he opened it, Frank Danson walked in. His face was pale, his eyes haunted.

'I've driven down from Allerton Cemetery.' He spread his hands helplessly. 'Someone's been interfering with Jenny's grave.'

16

He sat on the settee, leaning slightly forward with his elbows on his knees. The glass was clutched fiercely in both hands, but he couldn't hold it still and the ice cubes in the inch or so of whisky jingled musically.

As if personally affronted by the intrusion, Satan thumped down onto the floor and retreated to the kitchen in a huff.

'Interfered with in what way?' I said.

Danson took a breath, let it out.

'The flowers are tipped over.'

'Is that all you noticed?'

'I put them there once a week. In a vase.' He looked at me. 'The vase couldn't fall over on its own.'

'But was there anything else you noticed?'

'The edge of the grave . . . ' He trailed off, and shook his head.

'I know what you mean,' Calum said, softening his Scottish brogue so that it came across as immensely soothing. 'There's a sort of rectangular thingy all the way round, usually in something like white marble — is that it?'

Danson nodded. 'I can't be absolutely

certain that it's been moved, but there are marks in the grass. Quite a bit of loose dark soil, and smears on the marble.'

Calum had brought the bottle and three glasses in when he poured Danson's drink. It was a small table. With the two coffee mugs, it was getting crowded. I eased matters by pouring two more drinks, handing one to Calum and taking the other for myself. I sat back, trying to look nonchalant. In the other chair Calum had put on the lazy face with the drooping eyelids and was stroking his beard.

'If the grave's surround *has* been moved, it'll have to be reported.'

Danson looked at me. 'I know.'

'But before we take that step I think we should all go up there and take a good look, make absolutely sure.'

'If you like,' Calum said, 'you can stay here until we get back. Soak up some booze. Have a wee kip.'

'No.' Danson tossed back half the whisky, grimaced. 'No, that wouldn't work. It's a big cemetery, it's getting dark and graves are always hard to find . . . '

'But if you're right, somebody found it.' I watched him absorb that thought, and said, 'Have you noticed anyone following you?'

He shook his head numbly.

'OK. We'll all go, in my car.' I looked at

Calum. 'I'll make a quick call first, see what Sian's plans are for tonight.'

I keyed her number into my mobile and wandered through to the kitchen where the signal was always stronger. She answered at once.

'Sian, we're off out for a while. Frank Danson's here with us. Someone's been messing with his wife's grave.'

'God, no!' There was a breathy little silence. 'What does messing mean? You don't . . . you can't think someone's taken her body?'

'It's possible.' I waited while we both let the imagined horror sink in. 'All we can do is look. If it's serious, then Frank'll report it. We shouldn't be too long.'

'Be as long as it takes. I'll keep the settee warm.'

I felt a tiny prickle of excitement. 'You're coming over?'

'Just for tonight. A long sleep on a short couch, lulled by the nearby snoring of two weary PIs.'

I hesitated. 'And after that?'

'Then it's that sheltered accommodation we talked about — remember?'

'With me looking after you, always and forever.'

'Mm.'

'In a cave in the mountains worrying about bat shit and dead sheep?'

Sian's laugh was a rich gurgle. 'Who on earth said that?'

'Jemima Laing. On the only occasion I met her in the Sam Bone case. And now she's dead, never saw Bryn Aur, will never know how wrong she was.'

'I have, and do.' There was a moment's rich silence. 'But now you've got other deaths to look into, haven't you?'

'Or something — and we're ready to go.'

'So am I. I'll say goodbye to Meg, drive down and let myself in.'

'If you and Satan are asleep when we get back, we'll tread carefully. No stone unturned has a rider attached — always expect the worst — so it really could be a long night.'

*   *   *

I drove the long way round, cruising leisurely up Booker Avenue then along the arrow-straight dual carriageway of Mather Avenue. On the way, with the attack on my fragile person telling us that someone at the very least knew where I lived, Calum kept his eyes on the road behind. Traffic was sparse. There were headlights trailing in our wake, but one car blinked right at Heath Road and the other carried on when I turned up Springwood Avenue. From there to the cemetery gates on Woolton Road we were on our own.

Calum was pretty sure we had not been followed.

I parked with the wheels on the pavement, the car looking sickly under the sodium street light I had chosen for its probably false impression of security. The proximity of countless graves seemed to deaden all sound. A faint mist hung over the broad expanse of grass that made up Springwood recreation ground, and lights of every kind wore the haloes of a chill October evening.

Cemeteries are locked at dusk. We took one look at the heavy chain on the gate and went over the wall. Inside the cemetery the road went arrow straight for a while, but it was poorly lit. Darkness encroached on every side. The mist curled wraithlike around headstones and larger memorials to the ancient and modern dead that stood like massed ranks of troops waiting hunched in stillness for the morning light. I thought of Wellington, and how in the Peninsula he would hold his troops behind the crest of a hill to await the French . . . how he was wont to ride out after the rain . . .

And the rain now had stopped. I splashed through a puddle, heard Calum chuckle.

Then Frank Danson touched my sleeve.

'This way,' he said, and veered right.

He left the path and went swishing across wet grass. We blundered into a world where the long shadows of memorials fell before us to create patches of light and dark that tricked the eye. Uneven ground in pathways like irregular gridlines between the graves turned a stumble into a lurching fight for balance often gained only by clutching at cold damp marble and apologizing in a hoarse whisper to the unknown dead.

'Here.'

Danson had stopped. I saw a white headstone with two plump cherubs, the marble surround Calum had described enclosing a bed of chippings that sparkled. Near the headstone a heavy vase with a wide base was standing upright, the flowers a splash of colour.

'Been moved,' Calum said bluntly, edging along the base, using his foot to point to the long straight depression in the grass and the narrow V-shaped gap between base and headstone. 'It's cockeyed now, do you see?'

He was talking to Danson.

'Yes. I can now.'

'But has it been moved accidentally, do you think, maybe by council chappies cutting the grass and bumping it with the mower — ?'

'Or purposely moved right out of the way so that the people doing it could get at . . . what's underneath.'

At the hollow despair naked in his own voice, Danson shivered. There was an eerie, hard-edged rustling as he went down on one knee to brush almost reverently with the flat of his hand at the sparkling chippings. That simple task — no doubt performed at every visit — suddenly acquired especial significance: the chippings, too, had been disturbed; the sharp, flinty particles were stained and amongst them there were ugly clumps of moist soil.

'This was no accident,' I said. I watched Danson climb to his feet, his face haunted. 'If we report it there'll be more disturbance, men digging, the glare of spotlights taking away any privacy. But it can't be ignored, mustn't be ignored — because with this, with whatever it is they've done here, they've stepped over a line and gone from malicious harassment to out-and-out lawbreaking.'

'They crossed that line,' Calum said, 'when they sent thugs to kick the shit out of you.'

'Goes with the job, and this is not about me, it's — '

I saw the flash an instant before we heard the double crack of the shot and the bullet's impact. It smacked into one of the cherubs and ricocheted. Sparks flew. The chunk of lead whined into the night. Marble splinters hissed through the air.

Calum clapped a hand to his face. He ducked behind the headstone, softly cursing. I lunged, hit Danson with my shoulder and drove him flat onto the soaking wet grass. He grunted with shock.

A second shot cracked. The bullet hit the other cherub with a solid thunk. The head fell off and bounced off the vase. Danson saw it, made an angry, guttural growl deep in his throat and twisted beneath me. I leaned on him, held him down while six more shots cracked out. But now the marksman was aiming high. The bullets hummed harmlessly overhead.

Then we all heard a faint, distant laugh. Footsteps sped across grass, then onto the road. Faded. Were gone.

When Calum straightened, he was holding a handkerchief to his face. It was dark and shiny with blood.

★ ★ ★

Wipe away the blood, and sometimes it's difficult to find a wound. So it was with Calum. We returned to the Quatro and from the big first-aid kit I took enough gauze to wrap a mummy and with it mopped at the bearded face and uncovered one tiny nick high on the cheekbone. I applied a plaster and stepped back to admire my work in the unearthly sodium lighting. The bleeding had stopped, but before the staunching it had flowed south.

'Enter Red Beard the pirate, looking pained,' I said.

I was holding his shoulders, tilting my head to examine the patient. On the other side of the road a couple of merry gentlemen wending their way homeward wobbled along the edge of the recreation ground.

'Go on, give 'im a kiss,' one shouted, and the other cackled so hard he finished up on his backside in the grass. He struggled up, stopped his pal from rubbing at the damp patch on his pants with a clenched fist and an irate, 'Geroff will yer!' and they staggered on their way.

Danson, meanwhile, was struggling with mixed emotions as he watched the pantomime.

'Decision time, isn't it?' I said.

'No. We've got no choice.'

'We have in what we do before we take that step.'

'What can we do?'

'Well,' Calum said, 'a few moments'

thought about what we actually saw up there might be enlightening.'

I nodded. 'Mm. And the first thought is, there's not enough mess.'

'Exactly. Exhume a body and you'd have more than some dirty gravel and a few wee marks scraped in the grass.'

Danson was clearly puzzled. He frowned at Calum, then turned to me.

'You're splitting hairs. Something's been going on there, and it's up to the police to investigate.' He flapped his hands angrily. 'For Christ's sake, we've been shot at.'

'Which is why, if we're going to take another look, we do it now,' Calum said.

'Before the police respond to the phone calls that have undoubtedly alerted them.' I grinned icily. 'For want of a better word.'

Danson was still undecided. I was itching to do some digging and I knew Calum felt the same way. He'd already opened the boot and was searching among the tools. I didn't carry spades or US army entrenching tools, so the best he could do was a couple of tyre levers. He held them up to the light. I nodded.

In five minutes we were back at the grave. After the fusillade of shots we had left in a rush, but now Danson had time to pick up the cherub's head and dust it off. I could see

161

he was keen on more tidying up, so I grasped his arm.

'Leave everything until later.'

'I don't like it.' His face was tight, his eyes narrowed. 'It's wrong. It's illegal. Just what the hell are you going to do?'

'Mildly scrape.' My tone was reassuring. I looked across at Calum. 'That's about it, isn't it? Nothing more. Just move the chippings — or some of them — and go down a couple of inches.'

'Aye, and with all haste,' he said, dropping gingerly to his knees in the wet grass and leaning across the marble surround with tyre lever poised.

We chose a spot about a foot down from the headstone, four feet up from the foot of the grave, and began shifting the gravel from that couple of square feet. Don't ask me why. A woman would call it intuition, but as I'm a PI I'll have to put it down to another of those hunches.

Or maybe it was just common sense: when you're expecting to find a body, you don't start by looking for the feet.

Danson was an apprehensive onlooker, I was the labourer tidying up after the lusty Highlander. Calum scraped energetically and with much musical chinking of the tyre lever. Now and then he grunted at the awkwardness of his position, but I knew he was reluctant to step inside the surround for fear of hurting Danson's feelings.

In the end, it proved unnecessary. He was a mere three inches into the soil beneath the marble chippings when he stopped suddenly and cast a sideways glance in my direction.

I felt a clammy hand touch the back of my neck, shook off the ghostly feeling. The tyre lever was tossed aside with a clank. With both hands Calum carefully moved away the dark earth. He could have been an archaeologist uncovering ancient, brittle bones, but what was gradually revealed in the light of the rising moon was a thin pale face. The skin was wet, the colour of that white polystyrene membrane you find wrapping your new DVD recorder. They hadn't even closed the eyes. Black and sunken, they stared up sightlessly at the night sky without concern for the soil that clung like cheap mascara to eyelashes and thickly clogged their corners.

Danson had moved away. He was leaning against a tall headstone and I heard him harshly retching.

'James Cagan,' I said.

Calum nodded. 'It bloody well has to be.'

And we were both gazing at the face of the dead man who had been taken from the Royal's mortuary when the swelling moan of sirens announced the arrival of the police.

17

Time passed quickly, although it must have been fully an hour before the police had located the keys to the gates and finished what they had to do, and by then we were again getting drenched by a heavy drizzle. Initially things got a bit hectic. The police had come to investigate reports of a shooting only to be faced with the decomposing body of a small-time crook who had died a natural death then gone walkabout. He had quickly found a grave, but it was not his own; James Cagan in death had become a cuckoo, when in life — according to all I had heard — he had at best been a lame duck.

We were questioned by the uniformed police officers, together then individually; faced with two unrelated crimes — or perhaps no crimes at all — they seemed unable to decide how to proceed. Eventually they called for help, two plain-clothes detectives arrived and, after more questions, we were all invited to report the next day to write and sign formal statements. But it was clear to everyone there that the evidence on the ground made our statements almost irrelevant. The gunshots had been fired by somebody unknown and had caused no serious injury. The body buried shallowly in Jenny Danson's grave had been placed there by persons unknown; it would be returned to the hospital, and go from there to a pauper's grave.

While we were waiting for the detectives to finish questioning Danson, Calum and I walked down the road and, wet and cold, sat in the Quatro and talked idly about this and that. There was no urgency. Whither the investigation was going and how tonight's happenings changed things would be discussed later, so mostly we pondered on Danson and his state of mind. To both of us he had come across as a strong man caught in a horrendous situation. I had seen him stricken with grief at shocking images of kidnap; so tense in his own home that he couldn't sit still; angry enough to strike blows when I had thrown suspicion on his staff; and, tonight, driven to nausea by the discovery of a corpse which, quite possibly, had nothing to do with his troubles.

But Calum and I didn't believe that, not for one minute. I had latched onto Cagan through the most fragile of possible links, but tonight that link had become forged in steel; James Cagan had not been placed in Jenny

Danson's grave by happenstance: it was deliberate, and at last we had something we could get our teeth into.

Eventually they finished with Frank Danson and he came jogging down the slope to the road. We had been warmed by the car's heater; Danson's white hair was wet, his teeth chattering as much from nerves as from cold. I drove him home. We made sure he was in dry clothes and settled before a meaningless late-night TV show with a glass of strong whisky in his hand.

And so, at last, we went home to Grassendale.

Day Four — Thursday 13 October

'You were right about a long night.' Sian said. 'With sinking heart I just know it's about to begin.'

It was after midnight. In faded jeans, woolly jumper and bare feet she was stretched out on the settee with Satan like a crumpled black rug at her ankles, a mug of drinking chocolate clutched in both hands. Unusually, after slipping into dry clothes Calum and I had opted for the same drink. Maybe we too sensed a long session in the offing and knew that our usual brandy-laced coffee would make for muddled thinking.

Sian was pretty well up to date, at least with the events of the night. But she'd been elsewhere on a couple of occasions when Calum and I had discussed the case, so I knew there would be some gaps.

'So,' I said, 'getting down to brass tacks, I think we need first to establish just where we are.'

'To use a phrase to which we're no strangers,' Calum said, 'I'd say with confidence that we're no-bloody-where at all.'

'Ouch,' Sian said. 'Is it that bad, Jack?'

'In terms of how much help we've been to Frank Danson, yes it is. So if we really are no-bloody-where at all — how do we get some-bloody-where?'

'We juggle questions,' Sian said. 'Like, who is the woman who almost certainly master-minded the kidnapping?'

'Well, even that's now reduced from certainty to possibility,' I said. 'If we agree with Haggard — that there's a man or men involved — then even the mystery woman could have been a mere foot soldier.'

'OK.' Sian nodded. 'But we've still got to ask who she is, and find her. Then there's Calvin Gay. Was he involved? Is he still involved? And what about James Cagan, where did he fit in?'

'Right,' I said. 'No more questions, is that it?'

Sian thought for a moment. 'Mm. Yes, I think so.'

'If those are the questions,' Calum said, 'what about suspects, Jack?'

'For the woman involved in the kidnapping I'm looking at Becky Long, Ginny Felix and Claire Sim. All about the right age. All close to Danson for many years.' I shrugged. 'If they're clean, then unfortunately we have to start from scratch. The male suspect or suspects are thin on the ground. Both the men who snatched the kids are dead. Two possibles for the men behind the scenes are also dead: Fox and Cagan. Cagan was involved, but we don't know in what way. Calvin Gay is still there, but might not be involved. And, of course, as with the woman, it could be someone we haven't met or heard of.'

'Then you're ruling out Frank Danson?' Calum said.

I looked pensively into my cocoa, used the tip of a finger to shift some skin across the surface, and took a sip.

'I think I am. OK, maybe one day soon that'll come back to haunt me, but the idea that Danson in some way and for some reason got rid of his own sons without his wife's knowledge — or that they did it together and she later committed suicide because of a terrible remorse — no, I'm putting that right out of my mind.'

'You're beginning to like the man?'

I looked at Sian. 'Yes.'

'So he's innocent?'

'No. It's just that the whole idea's too frightful to contemplate, and I can't think of a single possible motive. I'll look elsewhere.'

'If the idea of him being involved is frightful, doesn't the same apply to Becky? Bloody hell, Jack, she's Jenny's *sister*.'

'I know. And although I don't like the idea, well . . .'

I shrugged.

'Which brings us,' Sian said, 'to clues.'

I sighed. 'Where the hell do we start.'

'By trying to come up with some,' Calum said, with a shake of the head, 'because I for one am completely stumped.'

'Well, we've got photographs, and that's a start.'

'Aye, and from those we've already identified two dead men.'

'Ah!' I lifted a finger. 'We have identified them, haven't we — or as good as, and I'd completely forgotten? Remember we talked about it before and said if we knew who the men in black were we could hunt down relatives or friends and ask questions? Well, I think I told you Willie Vine located them on the computer when we were discussing that tattoo. The records are there. A phone call should give us their names.'

'So a promising line of enquiry opens up,' Sian said.

'Yes, and now we *are* getting somewhere. But so far we've been dealing with things we know have happened, names we can trace, evidence we can look at time and time again. James Cagan is different. I haven't got a clue where to start.'

'How about with Claire Sim,' Calum said, and I clapped a hand to my forehead.

My obvious chagrin had Sian puzzled. There was a question in her blue eyes.

'I pinched a photograph of her from the KING OF CLUBS and took it to the hospital,' I said. 'A nurse identified her as the woman who was visiting James Cagan.'

'Goodness, and you haven't tackled her?'

'Not yet.'

'So that's our next step.'

For a short while there was silence as we basked in the warm glow of accomplishment and sipped our way through mugs of cocoa. The silence disturbed Calum's scarred black moggy. He opened one eye and yawned, then rolled, fell off the settee, landed on his feet and promptly lay down and went back to sleep.

'There's a big gap,' I said at last. 'Claire's here and now, but those blokes died twenty years ago.'

'As you suggested, the way around that difficulty is to approach Haggard and Vine,' Calum said. 'The names of those two dead men will provide us with a lead, and we'll have people to talk to.' He fussed with his beard, his eyes distant. 'But I'm thinking priorities here, the enquiries to make that are going to get the quickest results. I can dig into the kidnappers' pasts through Willie Vine, but isn't it a waste of time chasing dead men? I mean, if Sim and Cagan have got a history, you could talk to Claire and get close to solving the case with that one interview.'

'Mm. I think you're right.' I looked from one to the other. 'So, what has intelligent discussion given us? Sian, can you summarize?'

'The girls first, in order of priority,' Sian said. 'You question Claire Sim. If nothing comes of that you tackle Ginny Felix, then Becky Long.'

'How do you see Ginny? She was in the woods, remember, where dead bodies lay a-mouldering.'

'Yes, but she was carrying a camera.' Sian

shook her head. 'I'd be inclined to dismiss her. She works at a photo agency. She was probably polishing her skills in the hope of a move up the ladder.'

'Or the camera could have been a handy prop to disguise her real intentions.' I shrugged. 'Sorry, go on, Sian.'

'OK, well, I'm not too sure about Calvin Gay — although through him you might finally eliminate Bill Fox.'

'And the two dead kidnappers?'

'Last resort.'

'I notice you've been saying 'you', meaning me. What am I, the Lone Ranger?'

Sian smiled. 'I,' she said sweetly, 'will be busy sorting out my sheltered accommodation.'

'My sainted aunty,' Calum said, 'are you two finally getting your act together?'

'What's good for the goose . . . ' I said, pointedly, and Sian cocked her head at Calum.

'Am I missing something of importance here?'

'You were absent when she visited, but, aye, there's a wee lassie called Georgie who's taken up what you might call pole position in my affections.'

'Have you noticed how, when he's embarrassed, he puts on the Scottish accent and falls back on gobbledygook?' Sian said, winking at me.

'I've noticed he hasn't yet answered my Lone Ranger question — '

'Because I, in addition to indulging in some pleasurable dalliance, must push on with those damned, pompous 15th Light Dragoons.'

' — and adopts a stiff-upper-lip accent when cornered. Yes, get on with the soldiers, Cal, but in the evening I'd like you to talk to Ginny and see what she *was* doing lurking in those woods. If Sian's right we can quickly rule her out. Also, I think we should bring Jones the Van into this.'

'To do what?'

'Watch Becky Long. Round the clock.'

Sian frowned. 'Why her? Christ, she's Jenny's sister.'

'I know. And your summing up really was helpful. Claire's priority, Ginny's a maybe — but Becky *was* a suspect twenty years ago. She's an ex-cop and there's something about her, I don't know ... anyway, I'd like somebody outside her house, checking on her movements.'

Calum nodded. 'Starting when?'

'In the morning.'

'I'll call him now, get the wee bugger out of bed.'

And so, for Sian and Satan at least, a long night that had turned out to be shorter than expected was already over. The two of them bedded down on the settee, Sian covered by a spare duvet, the black moggy outside it but wallowing in the heat from my Soldier Blue. I'd like to say that I went to bed too, but even as the meeting broke up I saw in Calum's black eyes that the reasonable amount of fruit it had borne had left untouched those aspects of the case that were supposed to be boy things.

I laughed inwardly at that, remembering the conversation with Becky Long and my assertion that, in the modern world, woman things had become man things. The same, of course, could be said for the reverse, and there was surely no one more able to cope with violent assault than the young woman who had reversed the norm — unfulfilled, she had walked away from the British Army in search of adventure.

Nevertheless . . .

Sian slept. Calum and I talked in the kitchen in darkness mellowed by the glow from lights dancing on both sides of the Mersey, the only sounds distant night noises and the soft hum of the fridge.

Others came when Calum clinked the rim of my glass with the bottle's neck and poured me a drink, then topped up his own glass and scraped his chair softly as he sat down.

'Vicious bastards,' he said. 'That's clear from those early photographs.'

'So we shouldn't be fooled by a couple of swinging boots and half-a-dozen rifle shots aimed to frighten, not kill.'

'No, and we must ask ourselves — putting a great deal of thought into the answer — what the bloody hell is going on, how dirty is it going to get and should Sian or any other woman be a part of it?'

'Georgie's not in yet anyway, and Sian will be in North Wales for at least the next couple of days. I'll slip down there when I get the chance. But as for how dirty it'll get, I'd say as dirty as it takes for them to' — I thought, nodded slowly and said — 'to get their revenge.'

'Well now,' Calum said, 'and from where did that idea spring?'

'Subconscious working overtime?' I shrugged. 'I think it stemmed from this: Danson would deny it — has denied it — but twenty years ago, perhaps for some time before that, he or his wife must have trodden on someone's toes and made them very, very angry.'

'Angry enough to hit back hard.' Calum

was intrigued, visualizing that person's fury and slipping inside their mind as they worked out how to cause the most pain. 'They watched him closely over a period of time, learned all about his family and made their plans. Then without laying a finger on him or his wife, they hit where it hurt; coolly and casually, without fuss, they walked in and snatched his two young boys from their warm beds. Never to be seen again.' He shook his head, his face bitter. 'But for some damn reason it didn't end there. They made Danson wait — made damn sure he knew he was waiting — until now. Twenty long bloody years.'

'But why now?' I said softly.

'And if kidnapping two kids and making them disappear off the face of the earth was only the beginning, how in God's name is it going to end?'

'With Danson's death,' I said, and Calum shot me a glance.

'And what about his kids? Dead? Alive? Will he see them again?'

'Perhaps. But not in the flesh. I think there'll be another photograph.'

'Aye, there's a pattern there somewhere, if only we could see it. But if that photograph doesn't come then we have to tackle Danson again — and no doubt hit a brick wall when we get the same answers.' His eyes were narrowed, his brow furrowed with thought. 'You know, we can't ask his wife, because she's dead — but surely one or both of them will have surviving relatives, and relatives very often have long noses and sharp eyes.'

'The list grows.'

'It was never going to be easy.'

'I'm not complaining. Growth is progress.' I sipped whisky. 'What did Stan Jones say?'

'Round-the-clock surveillance has been agreed.'

'Mobile phones and a rusty white van.'

'Aye, well, undercover investigators must blend with their surroundings.'

'Becky Long lives in Woolton, not Toxteth.'

Calum chuckled. 'Stan's playing it crafty. He's got some of that magnetic lettering stuck on the van. He's now a plumber, and parked where he can be afforded.'

After another lengthy silence in which the level of whisky in the glasses was lowered and eyelids began to droop as night pressed heavily, Calum came back with what, for that night, was the last word.

'They may be going about it in a very peculiar way,' he said through a yawn, 'and you may have your doubts, but when you consider the messages on the cards it's quite possible that whoever's out there really is preparing to return the missing boys to Frank Danson.'

18

Despite the late night we all started early the next morning. Sian had an overnight bag and odds and ends to collect from Meg Morgan's flat and she set off in the Shogun a little after eight to catch the Welsh DS before she went to work. From there Sian would head for North Wales and Bryn Aur.

Calum and I watched her go then ate a quick breakfast and I drove us to Admiral Street nick for nine. I guessed the routine taking of statements wouldn't involve Haggard or Vine, and I was right. From an upstairs window they watched us come in, but we were dealt with in an interview room by the detectives who last night had been called to the cemetery.

And it *was* routine. Danson had got there before us, and the three of us told the same story because it was the truth — or a very slight variation of it: Calum and I had gone to Allerton cemetery with Frank Danson because he believed his wife's grave had been disturbed. We discovered unusual markings and, without any intention of going further, had scraped away the gravel and some surface soil. Barely covered, we had found the body of a man. While at the grave we had been fired on by a person with a rifle. The grave's headstone had been damaged. We were unharmed.

Routine it may have been, but questioning and paperwork took more than an hour. We stepped out of the police station to a crisp clear morning of blue skies and bright sunshine, Calum caught a taxi back to Grassendale and the waiting 15th Light Dragoons, and Danson and I went to our respective cars for the trip down town.

I had neglected to tell Danson where I was going, and he looked up in some surprise when I walked into Danson Graphics half an hour later. The shock *I* got came from seeing the empty desk in the outer office. Ginny confirmed what I'd immediately assumed: Claire Sim had not turned up for work.

'Did she phone in?' I asked Danson. He was also in the outer office and had been looking at images on one of the light boxes. 'Or did you give her two days off?'

'Just the one.'

He was still uptight from coming into unaccustomed close contact with the police twice within the space of twelve hours and memories of a hail of bullets whining over the grisly remains we'd discovered in his wife's grave. But I knew he was also recalling giving me Claire's address. I watched him sit back, tap the light box nervously then swing to face me.

'I told you I trust my staff. What did you say to frighten her?'

'What she said to me, and what I later found out, suggests your trust is misplaced.'

'Rubbish.'

'No. She told me that between the dates I'm interested in she was visiting her mother in hospital. That was a lie: her mother's been in Spain for a month. To confirm my suspicions I took her photograph to the hospital. She was identified as the mystery woman who had been visiting James Cagan.'

I saw the shock hit him. In the sudden silence I could hear a clock ticking and the soft scrape of a chair from the inner room. Behind her desk Ginny was keeping quiet, probably on pins trying to remember what she'd said to me. Danson would know I'd also visited Ginny, but was biting his lip and saying nothing while she was in the room. And as all these thoughts raced through my mind I was aware that Stan Jones — Jones the Van — would by now be parking his rusty van somewhere close to Becky Long's house in Woolton.

'Claire may have lied to cover something

completely innocent,' I said. 'The first time I was at the hospital a ward sister told me Cagan had been visited by his sister. You'll know Claire's maiden name. Could that be right?'

'No. Her name wasn't Cagan.'

'All right. I'll see what I can find out.'

That would come as soon as I left Danson Graphics. But I wasn't quite finished.

'Frank, I took the latest photograph to a couple of police contacts. They checked through the records. I'm sorry, but those two young men were murdered very soon after your boys were taken.'

His face was wooden. 'Maybe now you can tell me why you were so certain they weren't my boys.'

'There was a tattoo. It was visible when the two men were photographed in your house holding Peter and Michael, and absolutely clear on the latest picture.'

He said nothing. His lips were pursed. I knew he was holding back strong emotions.

'The trouble is,' I said, 'their removal means I'm going to find it difficult digging up evidence from the past. You've been as much help as you can. So has Becky Long — I think.' I smiled to let him know I thought the opposite. 'However, I'd appreciate it if you could give me the names of relatives — yours

181

or Jenny's — who might be able to throw some light on what was going on twenty years ago — '

'No.'

'Are there any? Parents? Aunts, uncles . . . cousins?'

'Probably. Yes. But they're good people and I want them left alone.'

'You're blocking a promising line of investigation.'

'Not at all. Go back to the police. If you want relatives let them find the families of those two dead kidnappers. If you want information about killers, look in the gutter.'

I had no answer to that. I left, first asking him to be sure to phone my mobile if anything at all happened.

It was now eleven o'clock. As I drove out of the city and headed for Sefton Park and Claire Sim's flat I was wondering if the hard-eyed man who'd called to take her home from the KING OF CLUBS was her husband and if he knew of her unusual interest in James Cagan. And it had to be unusual. What woman would sit for hours on end at the bedside of a dying stranger? If he wasn't a stranger, why would she lie?

I was still no closer to an answer when I parked, climbed the stairs to the flat and knocked on the bright blue door. It was opened by Claire. She took one look and began to close it.

I jammed my foot in the opening.

'They've found Cagan's body,' I said, 'so it's me or the police.'

Her pretty face paled. Indecision flickered in her blue eyes, replaced at once by a look of determination. The pressure on the door slackened, but from her face I could tell that if I removed my foot she'd slam the door shut.

'It'll be easier with me,' I said quickly.

'Really? I'm so pleased.'

With an angry toss of the head she stepped away from the door and walked into the flat. I followed and clicked the door to behind me. For a moment I stood with my back against it, listening. Voices murmured, but it sounded like the television. In the small hallway a man's boots stood against the skirting board, and I was suddenly aware of the ache in day-old bruises. I went through with trepidation to a neat living-room with wide windows overlooking the sun-drenched park.

Claire was alone. She switched the television off and sat down.

I took her photograph out of my pocket.

'Give that back to George next time you're in the club.'

She looked at it and her lips tightened.

'So that's how you found out.'

'One of the nurses recognized you.'

She shrugged. She was sitting on one of those modern settees designed for the body to sink into. Right on the edge. It was a feat Sian would have appreciated. I sat down opposite her.

She said, 'There's no shame in visiting a dying man.'

'Then why lie?'

'Because what I do is none of your bloody business.'

'Forget me. You lied to Lee and Frank Danson.'

Her eyes roamed the room. She could have chucked me out with angry words, but she didn't. I said nothing. After a while the silence became unbearable.

'I had a good reason for being at his bedside.'

'With a micro-cassette recorder.'

She flashed me a startled look. I grinned.

'Nurses are trained observers.' I tilted my head. 'How were you involved with Cagan? What were you waiting to hear?' She said nothing. I said, 'You haven't asked me where Cagan's body was found.'

'All right — where?'

'He'd been buried under a few inches of earth in Frank Danson's wife's grave.'

She actually gasped. Her cheeks went pink.

'You see, that seems to prove that James Cagan was in some way linked to the kidnapping of Frank Danson's children. So you either tell me what you know, now, or I *will* be forced to bring in the police.'

She slid awkwardly off the soft cushions and crossed to the window. There was tension in her back, in the line of her shoulders. She was angry at the intrusion, the questions, probably wondering how little she could get away with telling me, how much she needed to say to get me out of the flat.

'I didn't know James Cagan,' she said, swinging to face me. 'That's the truth. I knew *of* him — I knew his name, because Ronnie worked with him.'

'Your husband?' She nodded. 'If you work with a crook,' I said, 'you're usually doing crooked work.'

'You might know about that — I wouldn't.'

'And you wouldn't tell if you did know.' That got no reaction. 'If Ronnie put you up to those visits — sent you there with a recorder — what did he want you to do?'

She made a little exclamation of disbelief. 'What do you think? He wanted me to listen, press the bloody record button if Cagan recovered consciousness and started talking.'

'If that happened he could have talked

185

about literally anything. Weren't you told to ask questions? You know, the right ones, the ones your husband told you to ask?'

She stayed stubbornly silent.

'Ronnie had to tell you something. Otherwise you couldn't know what he was after; what he thought you might hear.'

'That's right. I didn't.'

I sighed. 'All right, where is he? If you can't or won't tell me, I'll ask Ronnie.'

Her laugh was bitter. 'I wouldn't advise it. Anyway, he's away. I don't know where. He often shoots off.'

'So who took you home from the club?'

'A casual friend.'

'All right.' I stood up, dug around for a business card, handed it to her. 'Would you phone me if Ronnie gets back?'

She frowned, hesitating.

'One way or the other it's all going to come out — '

'Yes. All right.'

She showed me out. Her politeness told me she was probably a cut above her husband, a strong young woman caught between right and wrong, wanting the one but not sure how to reject the other.

I got back into my car with a feeling of satisfaction. Sian had been right. She'd placed Claire at the top of the list and a short conversation with that young woman had thrown up another name. Ronnie Sim, a man who had worked with James Cagan, and Cagan was connected to Frank Danson.

Before I drove away I rang Calum and told him the news. He gave me some in return. News from Jones the Van. Just after eleven, Frank Danson had driven up to Becky Long's house. Long had let him in. He was still inside.

19

On the way back to Grassendale I stopped off in Allerton Road for a coffee. Sitting in the café sipping a cappuccino and trying to eat a Danish pastry without sticking to everything I touched I gave some thought about what to do next.

Calum would be talking to Ginny that evening. Stan Jones was watching Becky Long and Frank Danson and would keep us posted. Clearly we needed to ask Claire's husband, Ronnie, some awkward questions — but he was out of town. Frank Danson had flatly refused to bring in his or Jenny's relatives so that seemed to leave me little to do but act on his parting advice: go to Willie Vine and, through records, trace the two kidnappers' families.

Easier said than done. The police were busy and I was still investigating the apparent resurrection of a twenty-year-old crime about which the victim — Danson — was still not complaining to the police.

I finished the coffee, went back to my car and drove to Calum's flat. When I got there he was not alone. The room was fragrantly scented. Georgie, in boot-leg black pants and a black polo-necked sweater was sitting in one of the leather chairs reading the latest *She*.

She looked up and smiled as I walked in.

'Hi, Jack. Care for a coffee?'

'Coffee with some of that, er — '

'Remy,' Calum mumbled through teeth clamped onto a brush handle.

'Would go down very well,' I finished, and grinned after her as she made for the kitchen.

Crouched over the soldiers with the Anglepoise picking out glistening grey highlights in his hair and beard, Calum listened with interest as I told him of my talk with Claire Sim.

'The name Ronnie Sim is not unknown to me,' he said. 'Small time crook, in and out of Walton and other prisons.'

'Well, we won't learn much more on that side of things until Ronnie returns. And I've got to rely on Claire phoning me when he does. Any developments at Becky Long's house?'

'Danson's still ensconced.'

'Just like us, snug as a bug.'

'Stan has binoculars. The bedroom curtains were swiftly closed when Danson arrived.'

'They could be talking.'

'Or practising origami.'

'There's only one thing she'll be folding,' Georgie said, returning with three coffees skilfully balanced, 'and that's her underwear.'

'Before or after?' Calum said.

'Well, as they were probably in an almighty rush . . . ' She looked at me and winked.

'And talking of debriefing,' I said, sitting down with my coffee, 'our bright new consultant was undoubtedly listening as I brought Calum up to date — so what does she suggest we do next?'

'Take a break.' She wandered over to the work table and rested a hand on Calum's shoulder. With the other she began stroking his neck. 'Leave town now. Help your lover move in.'

'My . . . lover?'

She grinned. 'Listen, you know what they say: when there's nothing happening, make it happen. You're right, I was listening. There's nothing you can do about this Ronnie feller until he gets back, and it's pointless going on a laborious hunt for those kidnappers' relatives when it may not be necessary. If you're being watched, whoever it is will see you leave. When you're conveniently out of the way, they'll act. You can bank on it. So . . . '

'Leave town.' I nodded. 'But that's risky. Photographs are one thing, but the people

190

we're hunting are getting more violent.'

'Calum's here.'

I grinned. 'Oh, well, that's all right then.'

That got a caustic smirk from Calum. He said, 'The violence is directed against *you*, my man. Its aim is to get you to lay off. If you leave town it's worked and we can all breathe a sigh of relief and relax. That includes the baddies. Georgie's right. With you out of the way they'll move on to the next stage of the Frank Danson saga.'

'And play right into our hands. Yes, all right,' I said, 'I'm going.' I looked at my watch. 'Just after one. I can be home by three. What about this evening, Cal? You're seeing Ginny. Are you taking our new consultant along for the experience?'

'Might be a bad idea.'

'Mm. Could also lessen the shock to Ginny's system of having an unknown, untamed Highlander turn up on her door-step.' I grinned. 'Might be an idea if Georgie formed the advance party — '

'Didn't I hear you say you were going?'

I lifted a hand. 'I'm gone.'

And without more ado — other than to grab the manila envelope of photographs and my toothbrush — I was.

* * *

The Liverpool drizzle of yesterday had been the tail end of a prolonged downpour that had drenched the mountains of North Wales, washing crags and scree and endless grassy slopes and winding roads, and leaving the air sweet and clear for today's brilliant sunshine. At this time of year when the sun is sinking in the west a drive in that direction usually calls for sunglasses, a flipped-down visor and a stretched neck to avoid driving into a tree, but early in the afternoon the sun was still high and I drove blithely and without haste and bounced the Quatro across the stone bridge into Bryn Aur's oak-shaded yard as I was switching off Classic FM's three o'clock news.

I parked behind Sian's Shogun, with thumping heart strode past the heavy pot of azaleas beneath which the spare key was hidden and kicked my shoes off in the porch, took a couple of swift strides and flung open the door to my big living-room. And stood there, dumbfounded.

No Foreign Legion barracks, this!

Heat wafted out to meet me. In the stone depths of the inglenook a wood fire blazed in the iron dog grate, logs crackling, yellow flames leaping and dancing. Although it was three o'clock and the mid-afternoon sun was bright, anyone who has dwelt in a cottage in the high country will know that bright doesn't guarantee warmth and the small windows of yesteryear make for early dusks. But today the impending gloom of those too-early October evenings had been beaten back by switching on red-shaded wall lights, and their glow was caught in the sheen of huge smooth slate tiles to turn the floor into a sea of warmth where scattered Indian rugs were islands of comfort tempting bare feet.

Sian was stretched out on the chesterfield. Naked amusement was dancing in blue eyes that yet managed to smoulder. On the coffee table a bottle of dark Merlot was open and in a fine crystal glass the wine was blood red.

I crossed that warm sea feeling like a marauding pirate lusting after the comely wench who rose to meet me, caught the trace of perfume I knew so well, stopped for an instant to drink in the sight of my Soldier Blue in a housecoat of many rich hues that were all put to shame by blonde hair that, released from its customary elastic band, fell over her shoulders like fine spun gold.

Then she was in my arms and careless of fine crystal or red wine we had fallen onto soft leather that whispered an invitation and, as I sank into perfumed warmth and a moist and billowing softness that was the rare, true Sian Laidlaw, all that mattered was the here and the now which had been so long in coming.

Day Five — Friday 14 October

You want me to fill in the details, tell you how we passed the time from three o'clock that afternoon until the cockerels crowing on the farm beyond the ridge dragged us from sleep at pink dawn the next day?

Forget it.

And that's not me being a spoilsport, it's me being practical: I don't remember. Hours had become a pleasurable blur — a description which is a massive understatement and would be justifiably mocked by wordsmiths like Willie Vine. Nevertheless, to use modern idiom I'm sure you'll get my drift — and even that's probably outdated and wrong!

Of breakfast I have but a vague impression. Then, somewhere between pushing back greasy plates and topping up coffee mugs, the conversation regained some kind of common sense and we established that Sian was here to stay; we laid some basic ground rules for two adults sharing a house and, for a while, contemplated the long term implications. Long term? Across the table we clasped

194

hands like childhood sweethearts but each of us recognized in the other's eyes an awareness that such happiness is fragile. Promises are all too often made meaningless by circumstance. Or, as Calum's countryman would have it when he was waxing lyrical about timorous beasties, 'the best laid plans of mice and men . . .'

★ ★ ★

At ten o'clock, Alun Morgan's Volvo estate came rattling across the bridge and rocked to a standstill under the big oak tree. The dishes had been washed and stowed away and Sian had gone upstairs to shower. Alun knocked on the front door. I yelled for him to come in and wandered into the living-room to meet him wondering, with natural scepticism, if it was a chance visit.

'I'd have walked straight in,' he said, 'but with two cars parked that close together and no sign of life inside the house I thought perhaps there was a message there to be read and acted upon . . . ' The shadow of a smile crossed his thin lips and his dark eyes glinted. 'Or maybe there was no special significance and it was just you parking in a bloody hurry so that you could gallop inside — '

'Who's been talking?'

'Wick rang me an hour ago.'

'With a message for me?'

'That's one reason I'm here, yes.'

'Give me the second one first.'

'Maybe Wick's is the second, and mine priority — but, either way, some of that special coffee you dish up would do wonders for a man feeling the after effects.'

'What was it last night, the Bethesda policeman's ball?' I grinned. 'Come on through, you poor sod.'

In the kitchen I started work on the percolator while Alun leaned against the draining board to look across the yard and down the slope to my stone workshop. Out of the corner of my eye as I poured water and spooned in the coffee I could see him nodding in a slow, speculative way, and I knew he was mentally juggling words. Maybe doing a bit of translating while they were in the air, because the language he favoured was Welsh.

'In there, were you, when Maguire came calling?'

He turned away from the window as I crossed to the Aga, a line of damp from the draining board across the front of his trousers.

I nodded. 'I usually am when I'm in residence. Slaving over a hot melting pot to keep Wick occupied.'

That amused him. But only for a moment.

'Academic now, isn't it? Maguire'll not be needing you again seeing as we've made an arrest.'

I stopped, the percolator poised over the hotplate.

'What, for both murders?'

'Maguire's wife, and Bill Fox. Same man.'

I plonked the coffee pot down.

'Bloody hell! So, who is it?'

'Calvin Gay.'

'Oh, come on!'

I sat down heavily at the table as Sian came through from the living-room, hair dark and damp from the shower.

'Alun,' I said, 'has just snatched a suspect out from under our noses.'

'Yes, I caught the last bit. But murdering two people now surely doesn't rule out snatching two kids twenty years ago.'

'God, don't complicate matters.' I looked at Alun as he dragged a chair out and sat down. 'What's his motive?'

'He denies everything, of course. But we'd already discovered Bill Fox and Patricia Maguire were having an affair, and we reckon Gay couldn't have that because *he* wanted her. There was a letter from him in the woman's jacket pocket, threatening her and so incriminating him; Gay was daft enough to leave it there. Faced with that and his presence at the conference in Betws — '

'I spoke to him. He talked as if only Fox and Maguire went there.'

'Oh no. He was there all right, and his fingerprints were on the old Heckler and Koch P9s we found in what I suppose you would call the vestry in that mission of his.'

'So he's a murderer. Doesn't that make him more rather than less likely to fit into the Frank Danson case?' Sian said.

'No.' I shook my head and watched her take the bubbling percolator off the Aga and pour coffee. 'The Danson kidnapping was well planned, and it ain't over; this was murder in hot blood, no plan at all.'

'Yes,' Sian said, 'but we've agreed that if a woman planned the Danson kidnapping, she needed a man for the muscle.'

She put down three steaming mugs. I went to the cupboard, found the Remy, gurgled a stiff tot into two of them. We all sat and savoured our drinks. Sian was right, but I was still inclined to rule out Gay. Gut feeling again. If he *was* involved in the Danson case then surely the female *Kapitan* would have restrained him, vetoed any crime of passion.'

Which reminded me.

'What was Calum's message, Alun?'

'The young woman he spoke to last night

admitted everything.'

'Everything — as in what?'

'She was up there in the woods, some time before Gay was committing murder. She had a camera. Your Frank Danson has a competition on his web site. She's entered. If she wins, or gets short listed, she'll ask to be promoted to camera-woman. Or is that camera person?'

'Photographer.' Sian smiled sweetly.

'That's it,' Alun said. 'Another of your suspects crossed off the list, according to Wick.'

'One from low down the list,' I said. 'As, I suppose, was Gay.'

'In this case,' Sian said, 'there are very few hot suspects.'

'Nor cold ones. It's supposition all the way, me adding cards to the top, someone else sneaking in to deal them off the bottom.'

'You do still have Ronnie Sim,' Sian said. 'Remember, Claire's husband, who's out of town.'

'Out of circulation,' Alun Morgan said. 'The Ronnie Sim I know has been locked up in Walton for a year, with God knows how long to go.'

'Damn!' I said bitterly. 'I'm beginning to wonder if anyone's telling me the truth.'

★　★　★

Alun Morgan finished his coffee and left in his smoky old Volvo to deal with Gay down at North Wales Police Headquarters in Colwyn Bay. Sian donned lightweight boots and walking gear and, with a small pack loaded with waterproofs and emergency kit, headed for the hills. Glydyr Fawr was some 3,000 feet. For Sian, a gentle walk in the park.

I took a second cup of coffee through to the office. To say that the Danson case was in tatters was an exaggeration, but I couldn't believe that I'd lost two suspects in the space of an hour. Or was that three? — Ginny, Gay, Ronnie Sim. And in any case, couldn't losing them be a bonus? In the Sam Bone case I remember Calum saying that whichever suspect was left standing after the rest had died had to be the guilty one. Maybe that's what was happening here.

At my desk I spent half an hour catching up with Magna Carta paperwork then phoned a couple of toy soldier customers who had queries about the latest models. One was Tony Macedo, a member of Gibraltar Model Soldier Society. I'd last seen him near the end of the Sam Bone case when I'd been hunting down a suspect and had personally delivered Tony's order. He had now paid for a set of the 15th Light Dragoons Calum was working on, so my next call was to Liverpool.

'Almost finished,' Calum said, and I heard the liquid jingle of paintbrush against jam jar. 'Did Alun get to you yet?'

'Mm. And told me the tale. If Ginny's genuine then, sadly, another suspect bites the dust. Also, Calvin Gay has been arrested for the murders of Fox and Pat Maguire — and Claire's beginning to look complicated. Not less likely to have some odd stains on her character, but stains put there in a different way. Ronnie Sim has been in prison for a year. That seems to clear him of any recent connection to James Cagan, but it also poses the question of who sent Claire along to the hospital for a week-long vigil.'

'If you think she's complicated,' Calum said, 'wait until you here the latest.'

'Ah! Go on, enlighten me.'

'Our mobile surveillance unit phoned in.'

I chuckled at the image but, knowing who was being watched, my mind was racing.

'Stan the Van,' I said. 'A canny wee man, and he's come up with something — right?'

'Absolutely. That canny wee man has told me that after Frank Danson arrived at Becky Long's there was no further movement. The bedroom curtains remain closed. Danson has yet to emerge.'

'Well now, that is interesting.'

'Raises a number of possibilities. Allows us

to mention those unmentionables.'

'A father being responsible for the kidnapping of his own sons. Plus the sister, Becky Long, being the woman in the case. Mm. The first has at least been mentioned — I ruled it out — the second has always been a possibility.'

'But now?'

'Now I think I need to have a serious talk with Frank Danson. How does Stan feel about . . . Hang on a minute, Cal.'

I was up and looking out of the window as another vehicle came bouncing across the bridge, this time with much rattling of panels. An old Land Rover. Which meant only one thing.

'Gwyn's just driven into the yard,' I told Calum. 'Before you go, I was about to ask how Stan feels about maintaining his vigil.'

'He's eyeballing Long's house while working his way through *War and Peace* from page one. Probably good for another day.'

I chuckled. 'Good. Tell him onward and upward.'

I put down the phone, yelled, 'The door's open, Gwyn,' and went through to the living-room.

20

In the years that I'd known Gwyn Pritchard I'd grown hardened to the gaze of grey, intelligent eyes that would watch me shrewdly and unblinkingly in the manner of the eagles that once soared over the heights of Snowdonia. Recently that gaze had softened, and I liked to think it was because of the help I had given him in finding his wife's killer as much as from the mellowing that comes with old age.

Often he called in on the way to market, for Gwyn still dabbled in sheep farming on the slopes tumbling down from Moel Siabod. Sometimes it was simply for a chat, and I had never known him to refuse a mug of the brandy-laced coffee for which I was justly famous. Or perhaps that should be infamous.

Today he had been passing. Tootling along in his battered Land Rover at thirty miles an hour he had taken the turn off the Bethesda road and now was quiet but content, and in no hurry. We sat in the living-room, me on the chesterfield, Gwyn on a harder chair close to the inglenook and iron grate in which the ashes of last night's crackling log fire lay white but not quite cold, sipped coffee that brought a faint pink flush to his weather-beaten cheeks and talked of this and that which inevitably touched on the investigation into his beloved Myfanwy's murder before moving on to the latest mystery.

And then I had an idea.

'I've got something you might recognize,' I said, and leaped from my seat to find the manila envelope I'd brought with me from Liverpool. It was under the coffee table where it had fluttered and been forgotten in last night's tempestuous coming together. I gathered it, opened the flap and took out the 10″ × 8″ print showing two small boys playing in a garden.

I passed it to Gwyn.

'Right,' I said. 'Where's that?'

The grey eyes, it seemed, were not that sharp. He fumbled in the pockets of his green waxed jacket and pulled out a pair of wire glasses that rested like looped and knotted black cotton on a nose broken more than once in a club-rugby rolling maul. Through them he examined the photograph. He took his time, hmphed once, then nodded and allowed himself a smile.

'That would be the Jones place on the Dolwyddelan road.'

'Jones?'

He nodded.

'This is Wales — and there's only the one Jones?'

'On the Dolwyddelan road, yes. One or two in other parts, I believe.' This with a straight face. His eyes innocent.

'Has it got a name?'

'It has.'

'So what's it called?'

'The Jones place.'

'Ah.' I nodded. 'And there'll be someone living there now?'

'Oh, yes.'

'Called Jones?'

Gwyn smiled. 'Smith.'

'Honestly?'

'Gospel.'

★　★　★

I waited until Sian returned from her mountain hike, and together we left for the Jones place.

To get to the Dolwyddelan road meant driving to Betws-y-Coed, continuing on through the village then swinging right once Waterloo Bridge had been crossed then right again a short way up the A5. Then it was a bit of a wriggle through tight bends around a beauty spot known as the Fairy Glen before the road became more manageable and Sian was able to concentrate on navigation. She was holding the photograph. I thought we might have passed the house. The Jones place. Sian thought not.

'Too steep and wooded back there,' she said, waggling the print. 'On this the location seems flattish — and behind the house there's open land and then a hill.'

We found it after another mile and without too much difficulty: it was the only house in sight, the stone wall fronting the road was unchanged, the sloping garden unmistakable and all so familiar I expected to see the same two boys playing there.

Danson's boys. He believed it, and so did I.

I pulled the car tight onto the grass verge. That put me up against the wall, and I climbed out on Sian's side as a cattle truck rumbled by. The heavy wooden gate creaked. When we knocked on the door a young woman answered. Too young. Unless, of course, she was the daughter of the people who lived here almost twenty years ago.

Sadly, we were out of luck.

'We bought it a year ago,' she said, standing in the doorway, the sound of a television in the background.

'What about the previous owners — had they been here long?'

'A year. They got sick of the cold and were emigrating.'

I smiled. 'I know the feeling.' I took the photograph from Sian. 'It's a long shot, I know — but do you recognize these boys?'

She looked at it, and shook her head.

'This was before the extension was built' — she pointed to the side of the house — 'and that's been up ages.'

I hesitated. 'And you've no idea who was here then?'

'Two owners in two years. A few more before that, I think.' She shrugged. 'I'm really sorry.'

We thanked her, and walked away. Back in the car, I looked at Sian with a grimace.

'Dead end.'

'No more than we expected.'

'Mm. But how d'you go about tracing previous owners?'

'Manny Yates might know.' Then she smiled. 'Of course, you could always ask your live-in assistant.'

* * *

Back at Bryn Aur we had an early lunch then did some forward planning. I was returning to Liverpool. Sian had wangled some work at Plas y Brenin Mountain Centre and, over the next few days, would be out on the lakes teaching ATC cadets how to paddle their own canoes, Canadian style.

But that started tomorrow. Today she agreed to go back to the Jones place and ask Mrs Smith for the name of the estate agent she had dealt with. I thought a call to their office might bear fruit. Sian went one better and said she'd also get the name of the Smiths' solicitor. Surely, she said, the names of *all* the owners would be on the deeds?

I watched her Shogun rock its way over the bridge, phoned Manny's office on the off chance but got his answering machine and left a message. Then I called Calum and asked him to tell Stan Jones to stand down. If I couldn't talk to Manny, I'd tackle Frank Danson — if he'd emerged from Becky Long's bedroom.

It took me just over the hour to reach Liverpool. The rain had started again, the spray kicked up by the traffic filming the windscreen. By the time I got to Long's house in Woolton the windscreen washer reservoir was empty.

There was no sign of life. The bedroom curtains were closed. I sat in the car, fingers drumming on the steering wheel boss. What was going on? Stan the Van had taken up his position, watched Frank Danson arrive, seen

Long let him in and soon after that someone had drawn the bedroom curtains. Stan had sat there all night reading *War and Peace*. Nothing happened. From the looks of it that was the way things remained — which was bloody ridiculous.

I took a deep breath, climbed out of the car, splashed through the rain and hammered on the front door. Waited. Hammered some more. No answer. I bent to squint through the letterbox, looked down a dark and empty hallway then put an ear to the flap and listened to the silence.

Was the whole house empty?

I glanced quickly around, saw nothing but dripping privet hedges and deserted gleaming pavements and sidled down the side passage to the back of the house. Downstairs curtains were open. There was nobody in the kitchen or rear living-room. Short of climbing through a bedroom window, I'd done all I could — and already I was soaking wet.

I got back in the car and drove slowly to Grassendale.

* * *

'So what d'you reckon, Stan?'

Mid-afternoon and inside Calum's flat it was, as Sian would say, like midnight in

Moscow. The rain had slackened to drizzle, skies were overcast, the room was lit by Anglepoise and table-lamp and outside the pools of light we were like three spies hatching plots against an unknown enemy.

'It's fuckin' obvious, isn' it? If they're not in the house they've gone somewhere else.'

'Yes,' I said. 'But where — and why?'

'Safeway,' Calum said. 'He's running out of milk.'

'Kwik Save,' Stan said, grinning. 'He's runnin' short of cash.'

'Or Liverpool airport,' I said, 'because he's running for cover.'

'Why?' Calum was openly sceptical. 'Do we suspect him because he spent the night with a woman?'

'Possibly,' I said, 'if he spent the night with a woman who is herself a suspect. And to get out without Stan seeing them they must have sneaked out.'

'Unless I fell asleep,' Stan said.

'You're joking!'

He glared at me. 'Have you ever tried *War an'* fuckin' *Peace?*'

'In a rusty van, on a dark night, rain drumming on the roof?' I shook my head. 'Not lately.'

'Changes things,' Calum said. 'Ring Danson's work, see if he's there.'

He wasn't. Graham Lee hadn't seen him since yesterday. And Claire Sim hadn't turned in.

'I'd say you're doing very well,' Calum said. 'Two of your suspects are dead. Three more are missing.'

'So you are including Long?'

'Just building a damning picture of unbelievable incompetence on the part of a PI who should, maybe, be down at the job centre.'

'I've got other work,' I said glumly. 'Which reminds me, how are the Dragoons?'

'Ready.'

'Then let's start packing.'

'Count me out,' Stan said. 'I'm goin' home for a well-deserved kip.'

'You kipped last night, and fucked up.'

'Jesus,' he said, sneering. 'Listen to the pot swearin' at the kettle.'

He left. Calum and I climbed with reluctance from comfortable chairs and prepared to pack Royal Dragoon sets in scarlet boxes. We didn't make it. We were standing there listening to Stan Jones's holed exhaust roar away into the distance when Frank Danson and Becky Long walked in.

21

'I'm being watched.'

'So am I. I've got bruises and bandages to prove it.'

'Isn't that part of your remit?' Becky Long said.

'That sounds like the official way of saying it's one of the risks that goes with the job.' I looked at Danson. 'But what's your problem with being watched? Surely someone's been doing that ever since the first card and photographs arrived.'

'Not openly.'

'Does how it's done make a difference?'

'I feel vulnerable. They're getting bolder.'

'Yes, they are. They used boots and fists on me so that I'd keep my nose out.'

They were sitting on the leather settee. Danson was his usual self with, understandably, a few more of the hard edges eroded by strain. Long had washed off the understated Goth image I remembered and was business-like in smart suit and flat shoes. I couldn't help thinking of the night of the kidnapping, and the woman who had walked in impersonating Long. Had that woman looked like this? Or was it, as others had suspected, Long herself playing a clever double game?

'Maybe they're getting bolder,' I said, 'because everything's going merrily for them and the end is in sight. Perhaps making you nervous is a deliberate softening up. It's certainly working. Is that why you and Becky spent the night together?'

'Jesus!' Long said, as my words struck home and light dawned. 'It's your man doing the watching.'

'Standard PI practice and good technique: if the baddies are watching you it's an excellent way of catching them.'

'If that's why you're doing it.'

I smiled at her. 'All right, give me another reason.'

'You suspect Frank.'

'It's possible. And now two suspects have cuddled up for the night and I'm doubly suspicious. Or perhaps I'm only suspicious of you, Becky. I remember when I first spoke to you I went into great detail about what was happening to Frank. Time wasted. You already knew, but said nothing.'

'There was nothing to say,' Danson said bluntly. 'And if you'd been doing your job you'd know by now that Becky and I have been close for a long time.'

'You were the one keeping it dark,' Calum

said. 'And being close and all that is no reason for us to dump the suspicions. Especially when you shut curtains in broad daylight and sneak away through a back alley.'

Danson shook his head impatiently. 'This is going nowhere. We sneaked out for a very good reason.'

'You were being watched by a scally in a rusty van.'

He smiled thinly. 'Yes.'

'But there's something else?'

Before he could say any more my mobile rang. I excused myself, left Danson and Long to Calum Wick's deceptively mild probing and went into the kitchen. It was Sian.

'Bingo.'

I grinned. 'Estate agent or solicitor?'

'Solicitor. I'm in Bangor. I've just left his office. He's holding the deeds to the Smiths' house. I fluttered my eyelashes and he went all weak and opened the safe.'

'Safe?'

'Well, filing cabinet, deed boxes, whatever.'

'And?'

'You'll love it. That photograph in the garden was taken when the boys were six or seven, right?

'Yes.'

'Which makes it about four years after the kidnapping; that's 1989. The man who owned that house then was a Gordon Merrick. The solicitor knew him well. He'd taken early retirement from his job and gone to live in Spain for four years. When he came back he bought . . . what was it? . . . the Jones place . . . and he moved in with his wife and two young boys.'

'Mm. Tallies with the photograph. They were Danson's boys, this feller had them and we've got a name. So where is he now, this Gordon Merrick?'

'Don't know.'

'And you can't find out?'

'No, but you can.'

'And you're going to tell me how.'

There was a chuckle over the phone. 'You'll work it out, no problem. Because the important bit I haven't mentioned is that, before he retired, Mr Gordon Merrick was a very senior Liverpool policeman.'

★   ★   ★

Could there be two senior policemen who retired at the time Becky Long was locked in a dispute with one prominent figure over her promotion? Of course there could. Did I believe that? Not a chance!

If there was a ghost of a smile on my face when I went through to the living-room, only

Calum saw it. I found a seat, saw Calum had done the same, and sat down.

'Right, where were we?'

'You were telling us that we're here because of something more than a scally in a rusty van,' Long said.

'Which was my way of putting a question,' I said. 'So why *are* you here?'

'First, let me ask you a question,' Frank Danson said. 'You've been in this from the very beginning. Everything that's happened you know about. With that knowledge I'd expect you to be thinking ahead, trying to second guess whoever we're up against.'

He looked at me expectantly. I nodded, knowing exactly where this was leading but content to let him ask his question.

'All right, so what are they playing at? What's their game. When they've played their last card — what's going to happen?'

'You'll meet your boys.'

Danson went still. It was the answer he'd been expecting. I could see it in his eyes. But still he was shocked.

'I agree,' Calum Wick said. 'That's what everything's been leading up to. The trouble is, we can agree the eventual outcome is a meeting but we haven't a bloody clue what their intentions are after that. You and your boys come face to face, but then what? Are

216

these nutters going to all this trouble just to hand them back to you — or what?'

'I don't think I'm foolish enough to believe that,' Danson said. 'But — for whatever reason — I, too, am convinced everything's leading up to a meeting and that meeting is not going to be on my terms.' He grinned wearily. 'That brings us to the real reason for calling on the two of you tonight.'

'You want to change all that,' I said. 'You want me to take the initiative.'

'That's right.'

'Which means getting to the boys when the kidnapper's not expecting it.'

'Kidnapper, kidnappers . . . ' He shrugged. 'Yes, right again.'

'Which means we've got to find them from a position where we really know nothing and have no clues.'

The enormity of the task I'd painted loomed large over Danson. His shoulders sagged a little. He sat back in the settee and nodded.

'Actually, that's not quite true.' I looked at Becky Long. 'I might know nothing and be short of clues, but I've come in twenty years late. You have the advantage of being involved from the beginning.'

She frowned. 'Meaning what?'

'All right, let's rule out suspect and assume

you're genuine. In that case, I think that from the very beginning you've had the knowledge that would have given Frank his kids.'

'You're out of your mind.' Her face had gone pink. There was fury in her eyes. 'Is this another go at saying I was the woman who walked in — '

'Into Danson's house?' I shook my head. 'No, I just told you, I'm *not* saying that.'

'Then what the hell are you saying? Look, Frank and I — '

'We've talked,' Danson cut in. 'Time and time again. We've had almost twenty years to beat our brains out, over and over again looking for something, anything that would give us the slightest clue — '

'And there's nothing,' Long said flatly, emphatically. 'Bloody hell, I was police then, in my thinking I always will be. Don't you think, given that, I'd've spotted something?'

'I'll repeat what I said: you've always had the knowledge. You just didn't connect what you knew with the kidnapping because there was no obvious link and the whole idea is preposterous.'

I looked at Calum Wick.

'Yet in another way it's all logical. Remember, Cal, our concern about how the boys — kidnap victims, headline news — could have been integrated into a family, if

218

that was one of the reasons for their being taken?'

He nodded. 'Who was on the phone?'

'Sian.'

'Talking from?'

'Bangor.' I looked at Long. 'Ever heard of Gordon Merrick?'

That knocked her off balance. I'd been blaming her for, perhaps unwittingly, withholding information that would have saved Danson years of grief. Now I'd switched to the police officer who had blocked her promotion. She couldn't see where it was leading and told me sharply to get off that track.

I shook my head. 'Frank, there was a house in one of the photographs. Your boys were playing in the garden. An old farmer, a friend of mine in North Wales, looked at the photograph and recognized the house. Now Sian Laidlaw has traced the deeds to a solicitor working in Bangor.'

I paused, not intending to, but knowing the news was momentous and would hit Becky Long with the power of a physical blow.

'Twenty years ago,' I said, into a sudden, hushed silence, 'that house was owned by Gordon Merrick.'

★ ★ ★

'Damn, damn, damn,' Becky Long said, through clenched teeth. Her face was white, her eyes huge. She reached for her cigarettes, fumbled, then flung the packet away.

'Time for a wee drop of something strong,' Calum said, and padded into the kitchen.

'It's all to do with that woman thing, isn't it?' I said.

Long nodded mutely.

'Where was it you went? An abortion clinic?'

'What bloody clinic?' Danson was bewildered. He looked at Long, who shook her head and fumbled for his hand, this time for her own comfort and reassurance.

'It was a place I went to twenty years ago when I walked out of that police conference,' she said, and squeezed his hand. To me she added, 'It was a fertility clinic. Merrick's wife was still quite young, but the treatment didn't work.'

'Ah.' I took a deep breath and nodded sudden understanding. 'Of course. They couldn't have children, and they wanted them desperately. It had to be something like that if they'd stoop to kidnapping another family's children — '

'No.' Long shook her head. 'OK, I didn't like the man and he was ruining my career because he was aware that I knew of his sterility — or her infertility, or whatever — and thought I'd . . . thought one day I'd spill the beans. But I knew Gordon well and I don't think he'd get his hands dirty. From what you've discovered it seems certain he must have agreed to the . . . the kidnapping, the handover, or *sale* of the boys, but somebody else did it, did it for him. Must have done. He wouldn't, he *couldn't* do it.' She looked at Danson. 'But he *was* a senior policeman. He'd have the money, and he'd know who to approach.'

I nodded. 'And he'd know the ins and outs of how to get new identities and everything else involved in suddenly, seamlessly acquiring two kids — when Danson's were still red-hot news — without arousing suspicion.'

'Doesn't matter!'

Danson blurted the words. He'd been bewildered but he was no fool and he was catching up fast. I knew he had rapidly come to the conclusion that talk of dirty tricks and police methods and a clinic where a woman's attempt to have children had failed was beside the point — and was wasting time.

'Doesn't matter if he planned everything, or if someone came to him out of the blue and offered him my boys for hard cash,' he said. 'He had them then, he may still have them now.'

'I'll find out. Calum and I will begin today, begin now — '

'How?'

I smiled. 'I'll make it up as I go along. But it'll be good.'

'Everything he does is good,' Calum said, walking in with four pungent coffees. 'Everything I do is better.'

The mood had lightened. It was dawning on Danson that through work he hadn't realized I was doing I'd presented him with a strong lead to the whereabouts of his sons — the first glimmer he'd had in twenty long years. Becky Long was still pale, still stunned with disbelief that in all that time she had never once got even close to putting two and two together. I thought she was being hard on herself — and she still had knowledge that could be useful.

'What does Merrick's wife look like?'

She shook her head, catching on at once. 'Too tall, too skinny — and she was too distraught at the time to mastermind a kidnapping and play the leading role.'

'So although we're a hell of a lot closer to tracing the two boys, the woman's still an unknown.'

'Aye, and she's the one we've got to worry about,' Calum said. 'If the two boys ended up with this Merrick character, he won't be the one playing games now. There's some other agenda here and we haven't got a bloody clue what that might be.'

Danson appeared entirely unfazed by Calum's downbeat assessment. He'd been absorbing punishing blows for almost a week, one shock on top of another slamming into him and sapping his strength as a nightmare from the past came screaming back to haunt him. Twenty years ago his sons had been kidnapped and the one slender thread of hope he'd clung to was a message telling him to wait. He was still waiting, but after the news I'd given him he was cock-a-hoop and, from the look in his eyes, I knew he was ready to meet head on whatever was still to come.

'What comes next?' he said now. His confidence had come rushing back to intoxicate. The tone was almost feverish. 'I hired you. You're the expert, the super sleuth — it said so in the *Echo*.' He grinned. 'So, go on, what's the next step?'

'Follow the one sure lead we have. We trace Merrick's present address.'

'And that,' Becky Long said, 'is going to be very easy indeed.'

Calum was nodding. 'He gets a police pension.'

'That's right. A regular cheque, so all his details will be on the computer.'

'To which you have access.'

'Through a friend.'

She took a mobile phone from her pocket and flipped it open.

'The kitchen's the best place for quiet and a good signal,' I said.

The door closed behind her. We all heard the faint beeping followed by the murmur of her voice.

Cautiously I said, 'This could go either way. I don't know when Becky last saw Merrick — '

'Never,' Danson said. 'She hasn't seen him since she walked out of that conference.'

'So he could be dead. He and his wife. Or living abroad.'

'The records won't have died with them,' Calum said. 'If he's abroad he still claims his pension. If he's dead it goes to the widow.'

'All I'm saying is, don't get your hopes up, Frank.'

'You're too bloody late, they're sky high.'

The kitchen door clicked open, catching us all doing some deep pondering. The phone snapped shut as Becky Long came back into the room. She didn't sit down. I think she was too excited. The phone was slipped into her pocket. She came up behind the settee and leaned forward to place her hands on Frank's shoulders.

'Gordon Merrick lives on the Wirral,' she said. 'I've got an address out in Hoylake. He's been living there for years.' Her fingers went pale as she squeezed Frank's shoulders, and I saw him shut his eyes like a man steeling himself for bad news.

'He's got two sons living away from the family home,' Becky said. 'Their name's are Cain and Abel — I wonder where that inspiration came from.' She took a deep breath. 'I couldn't find out where they're living — Scott will have to ask Merrick those addresses when he goes to see him. But my contact is quite certain they're both alive and well.'

22

Mid-afternoon had given way to early evening. Frank Danson had taken Becky Long home and I knew he'd stay in her small, comfortable house. Tonight both of them were in shock. It was no time to be alone.

Calum and I had finished packing the 15th Light Dragoon Guards and tomorrow we would label the boxes and get them off to the various overseas customers. I called Gibraltar and told Tony Macedo they'd be on their way. His genuine excitement and a sunny nature that seemed to bubble like wine brought brightness to a room that had seen too much gloom for one day.

'And with those wee buggers out of the way,' Calum Wick said as he stacked the last box, 'isn't it time we were heading for the seaside?'

'A phone call first would be — ?'

'Bad thinking. It's a touchy subject we're about to broach. We're going to tell an ex-policeman his criminal past has caught up with him, and he'll know he could lose two boys he's grown to love. How we're going to get anything out of him after that I really don't know. But I *do* know damn well that if he gets prior warning the drawbridge will go up, the portcullis will come down and the next thing we know there'll be boiling oil raining down on our heads.'

'In Hoylake.'

'Aye, well, I'm suggesting he'll object quite strongly when we start rocking the boat.'

Metaphors were still flying as thickly as arrows at Agincourt when we made our way down to the Quatro and I headed for the ring road, slipped through Queensway tunnel as easily as threading a needle — see what I mean? — and so sped towards Hoylake through rush-hour traffic that, once on the other side of the water, was all heading in our direction and slowing us down.

It didn't matter. There was a sense of urgency that was speeding up the pulse and tightening the breathing, but it was the urgency that always kicks in when there's a sudden breakthrough in a mystery that had seemed — well, too damn mysterious. It was an urgency that had nothing to do with any thought of Gordon Merrick slipping away before we got to his house, because as far as we knew the world he had created for two kidnapped boys had remained undisturbed for many years. There'd been no ripples on the pool of his life, if you really want another metaphor — which sounds bloody marvellous not to mention unbelievable, and bears no relation to reality.

When we got to Gordon Merrick's house in Hoylake, he'd gone.

★　★　★

The north wind was whipping in off the Irish Sea bearing the smell of salt and seaweed across Hoylake's nearby North Parade and driving ice-cold rain into my right ear. I was standing back on the kerb looking up at a three-storey house that was wet brickwork and blank unlighted windows illuminated wanly by street lighting that was obviously a council joke. Calum had gone round the back of the house with a torch. I heard the tinkle of breaking glass and fully expected to see the bearded Scot appear at one of the windows like Marley's ghost. Instead he came jogging back down the side driveway where grass grew wild and told me he'd put his foot through a cold frame and probably ruined Merrick's late lettuces.

He'd also raised the alarm.

Light flooded from the house next door as the front door opened. A man in a hooded jacket came down the path.

'What's going on?'

'We're looking for Gordon Merrick.'

He was a big man, grey-haired and wary. He stayed back behind his gate. With one hand he was holding the edges of his hood together against the rain. He had a mobile phone palmed in the other.

'I heard glass shatter,' he said. 'What did you do, kick the back door in?'

Calum laughed. 'No. Nothing like that. I think one of the local lads got careless and lost his bottle.' He gestured towards the house. 'There's nobody at home. D'you know where he is?'

'Yeah. He's in Spain an' I'm looking after the house.'

'So you'll have a contact number,' I said.

'That's right. In case there's an emergency.'

The implication was obvious and he wasn't budging. I dug in my pocket for a business card, walked over to him and passed it over the gate.

'We're looking for his two sons. We've got reason to believe they're in danger. I'd like to talk to Merrick, let him know what's going on.'

'You mean you're working for him?'

'No. I can't tell you who I'm working for. The point is Merrick doesn't know anything of this, so it's vital that I talk to him now.'

He hesitated. I could see him wondering if

there was any truth in my story, wondering if maybe he should phone Merrick first and ask him what was going on. He was teetering in that direction; it was just a phone call, after all. Then the weather made the decision for him. A fierce gust of wind snatched the hood from his fingers. Rain lashed his exposed face. He was getting cold and wet.

With a soft curse he flipped up the mobile, looked through the address book and came up with a number. I found another business card, scribbled the number on the back so I wouldn't forget it then thanked him and ran for the car. Calum was there ahead of me. I slid the windows down an inch to let in some air then found my mobile and keyed in the number. Spain was an hour ahead. It would be after eight o'clock. Too early for bed, but Merrick and his wife could be out on the town. I listened to the ring tone, willing him to come to the phone.

'Hello.'

'Gordon Merrick?'

'Yes.'

'My name's Jack Scott. I'm a private investigator.'

'Oh dear, I do think that ends this conversati — '

'Don't hang up! I'm trying to locate Peter and Michael — '

'Never heard of them.'

The phone clicked. The line was dead.

'Wrong names to throw at him,' Calum said.

'I know. It was stupid of me, I wasn't thinking. Two names and he's pulled up the drawbridge.'

'Maybe not. Get back to him. I think he'll be sitting there staring at the phone, scared rigid.'

'How much do I tell him?'

Calum chuckled. 'Other than those names, how much do you really know?'

I keyed in the number. Merrick answered on the first ring. I could hear him breathing; faint music; the clink of glasses.

'What do you want with me?'

I thought for a moment. Then I said, 'I don't have to tell you what happened twenty years ago because I've brought it all back to you by mentioning those names. But I'm talking to you because of what's happening *now*. All that time, all those years, one man has been waiting and hoping — and suddenly everything he thought dead and buried has come roaring back to life. But it's not that simple; it's not just between you and him.'

'You're talking nonsense. What happened twenty years ago was I retired from the police force. That's what happened, that's all that happened.'

'I know,' I said. 'Becky Long told me all about it.'

That shocked him into silence.

'Consider this: twenty years ago there had to be a third party involved or you wouldn't have got those kids. It's the same now. An unknown third party's involved. There are some nasty photographs. Links to a criminal who died in hospital. A grave has been desecrated — '

'Nothing to do with me — '

'I need those addresses.'

'I've got two sons. I don't know who it is you're talking about — this, what, Michael and Peter? — but if you're looking back twenty years, whoever they are they'll be grown men by now.'

'That's right.'

'Well, if you find them I hope they can help.'

'Two people were murdered in a North Wales forest. A man's body was stolen from the Royal Liverpool Hospital. It ended up in someone else's grave . . . '

I was looking at Calum. His hands were in his lap. He crossed his fingers; then his legs; then his eyes, and I bit my tongue hard and turned to look out at the rain.

'Then it's a matter for the police,' Gordon Merrick said, 'and I'm sure they're dealing with it.' He paused. 'Look, I'm flying back to the UK in a couple of days — '

'That may be too late.'

He took a slow, deep breath. I expected him to hang up again. He didn't.

'Why?'

'I don't know — and that's being honest with you.'

His chuckle was icy. 'And I'm supposed to believe a voice I've never heard before because it talks about being honest.' He paused. 'Give me a contact name.'

'You're wasting time.'

'You say you're a private investigator. If that's true you'll have contacts within the police force. Give me a name and telephone number.'

I looked at Calum. He'd been listening to the tinny voice in my ear. He shrugged, mouthed, 'Willie Vine'.

It was a number I knew well. I gave name and number to Gordon Merrick. He said he'd get back to me. Again the phone clicked in my ear.

'Pushing half seven and pissing down,' I said. 'Vine will have gone home.'

'Merrick's an ex-cop. If he could make two kidnapped boys disappear he'll have no problems getting Willie's home number.'

I sat nursing the mobile. Rain drummed on the Quatro's roof. Out of the corner of my eye I could see light flooding from the front door of the house next to Merrick's, the big man silhouetted in the doorway. If we stayed where we were suspicion would boil over and he'd call the police, or try to reach Merrick. But he wouldn't get through to Spain because Merrick would be on the phone chasing Willie Vine.

'You're asking a lot,' Calum said.

'Yes. Merrick brought two kids to manhood and now it's all gone pear shaped.'

'In his position would you play ball?'

'Hard to say. He'll be in shock. Twenty years ago two kids were kidnapped and somehow he got his hands on them — '

'We assume.'

'Assuming we're right, suddenly he's got a man on the phone who seems to know all about it and is demanding to know where those boys are living. If it was me I think I'd deny everything — which he did. Then I'd stall — which he did. Then I'd do what he's doing now: I'd check on the man making the call.'

'Unless,' Calum said, 'he's not actually phoning Willie Vine. Because if it was *me* on the other end of the line I think what I'd be doing is talking to those boys.'

'Jesus!' I said softly.

'Or is that me showing a wee bit of pessimism?' he said.

The phone rang.

Calum opened the car door and stepped out into the rain.

'Scott.'

'Somebody thinks highly of you, Shamus.'

'You must have got a wrong number.'

He chuckled. Suddenly he was more relaxed. I realized he could be making up the glowing references. Perhaps Calum was right and all he'd done was warn the boys.

'They live in Chester,' he said. 'Their names are Cain and Abel. They share a flat.'

He read the address to me. I juggled phone, pen, and the same business card and did some hasty scribbling.

'Go and talk to them,' Merrick said. 'They'll tell you what I've been trying to get across to you, but more forcefully. I don't think they'll be very polite. As for me I never want to hear from you again. If I do . . . well . . . let's just say you've been warned.'

On that sour note he left me. I slipped the suddenly dead phone into my pocket. The door clicked and cold damp air announced Calum's return.

'Where'd you go?'

'For a pee.'

'That must have amused our minder.'

'Aye. I went around the back of Merrick's house again just to get up his nose. Broke some twigs invading the shrubbery but switched off the torch for the sake of decency.' He grinned. 'He probably misconstrued my intentions, so if you feel like getting arrested just sit back for — how shall I put it — a wee while.'

I rolled my eyes. 'I'd love to, just to watch the fun, but we're going to Chester.'

I started up and pulled away from the kerb in an exhilarating shower of glittering spray that left yellowing dead leaves soaring and wheeling in our wake like jaundiced sea birds.

★　★　★

Spurred on by Calum's suspicious nature I stayed on the A540 and made it to Chester in fifteen minutes without getting winked at by a single speed camera. The car was buffeted by the wind, the trailing spray was straight out of a high-performance car video filmed on the edge of the Malibu surf, and I like to think that by the time I began applying the brakes — for the first time since leaving Hoylake — there were one or two more grey hairs being nervously tugged in Calum's beard.

The address given to me by Merrick was on the race-course side of the town, a block of private flats set back in tree-shrouded grounds with subdued down-lighters on low blond-brick walls and a glazed entrance that would have been noticed in Mayfair.

I swung in with the tyres hissing on the herringbone brick drive and was nearly wiped out by a black Volvo built like a tank but moving much faster. I caught a glimpse of two dark shapes in the back seat, was dazzled by light reflected from the driver's shades and closed my eyes as I drew to a stop in front of the building with Calum mumbling something that could have been a prayer.

It wasn't.

'That,' he said, 'was probably our boys making a dash for it.'

I grunted my disbelief. We climbed out, stretched like a couple of orang-utans in the steady rain and entered the building through revolving doors that whispered and gave access to a foyer with a reception desk against one wall flanked by chrome doors that I guessed were lifts.

Behind the desk a bald man in a smart uniform tossed a newspaper aside and watched us with stony gaze as we made wet footprints across his tiled floor.

'Jack Scott and Calum Wick,' I said, 'calling

on Cain and Abel Merrick.'

'So start callin',' he said, 'only make it fuckin' loud.'

I grasped the counter, rested my forehead on its cool surface then looked up at him.

'Please. Tell me that wasn't their slipstream rocking the car as I drove in.'

'That wasn't their slipstream rockin' your car.'

'But it was, wasn't it?'

'Yep.'

'So where have they gone?'

'Out.'

'Planned,' Calum said, 'or spur of the moment?'

'A woman called, they went.' He grinned at me. 'She called first.'

I leered. 'What was she like?'

He shrugged. 'Medium everything. Nondescript. Invisible in a crowd.'

'Colour of eyes?'

'Hidden behind shades.'

'Her first time here?'

'On my shift, yeah.'

'What about Cain and Abel on the way out? Usual merry selves or worried sick?'

'Impassive.'

I looked at Calum. 'Nondescript *and* impassive. He'll go far.'

'I do a lot of readin',' he said, and retrieved

his crumpled copy of the *Sun* as we walked out.

Back in the car I got the engine and heater running to combat the condensation rising from damp clothes, found a tube of spearmint Polos in the glove compartment and dished them out. Then I switched on the radio for the eight o'clock news and, with it murmuring in the background, began arguing with myself.

'A woman of medium build who wears shades on a dark night suggests the kidnapper has made her move. However, we have to consider your idea: Merrick phoned the boys then sent a minion to whisk them away to safety. On the other hand it may be neither of those but an ambitious middle manager who doesn't want to be recognized taking two eligible bachelors to a sleazy downtown nightclub.'

'It could have been their mother,' Calum said, 'if she wasn't in Spain.'

'Or their grandmother,' I said, 'if she's still alive.'

'Maiden aunt, cousin, a kinky friend in drag — '

'Wait, Cal!' I said, cutting in abruptly.

I was listening to Merseyside news.

'A young woman in her early forties has been found dead in a flat off Ullet Road.

She had been stabbed several times. Foul play is suspected. Police are anxious to interview a man who was seen twice at the woman's flat. He is described by the next door neighbour, who spoke briefly to the man, as tall, dark-haired, and in his early fifties.'

'Damn,' I said. 'She was next on my list.'

'Aye, but there are compensations.'

'My fame grows.'

'I was thinking infamy.'

'I need a miracle: something to bring her back to life.'

'Claire Sim. Our key witness.'

'Mm. She sat at James Cagan's bedside. Someone sent her to the hospital or she knew Cagan. I had to talk to her.'

'All is not lost. Cagan's dead, now she's dead. But someone knew both of them.'

'There's a thought,' I said as I slipped into gear and pulled away from blond brick and down-lighters and out into the traffic. 'All we've got to do now is find them — and that could take another twenty years.'

23

It was nine o'clock by the time we got back to Grassendale. While Calum rattled about in the kitchen making coffee I gave my Soldier Blue a quick call to bring her up to date with events, vicariously soaked up some misty mountain atmosphere brought close and intimate by her husky tones, then bade her a fond and reluctant farewell.

On the way back from Chester we'd temporarily shelved the idea of looking for people who might have known James Cagan and Claire Sim, although Calum had come up with one bright idea: Calvin Gay was a killer, but he was probably out on bail — or allowed visitors — and he had known Cagan. That might be worth a try, but not yet, perhaps not ever. First I had to talk to the police; I'd see Mike Haggard tomorrow. Tonight we'd call on Frank Danson and tell him what we'd learnt about his sons. It was quite possible that out of that meeting something would emerge to show us the way.

When we clattered down the stairs, stamped our way cruelly past Sammy Quade's flat and burst out into the damp night air, it was with a mild sense of optimism. We really were getting close. No matter what had happened subsequently, Merrick had come through with the address and, against the odds, we'd located Danson's sons. I opened the Quatro feeling like a man who's won . . . well . . . ten quid on the lottery, waited for Calum to climb in then pulled away from a River Mersey made oily and sullen by the persistent rain and so out onto the main road where traffic hissed and dazzled and, in a warm car wrapped in thoughtful silence, drove without haste to Woolton.

Becky Long's eyes narrowed with speculation when she opened the door to my knock.

'Trouble?'

'Some — and some progress.'

She stepped aside and we walked ahead of her into the living-room and found our way to seats. Light from a porcelain table-lamp with a lined yellow shade cast a warm glow, mellowing the ornaments and adding a touch of gold to enrich Frank Danson's whisky.

He was sitting in one of the living-room's deep chairs. Warm, relaxed, no sign of tension. Nothing about him to suggest that the police had just left after delivering terrible news, so I knew he hadn't heard about Claire. And if I'd expected shock at our arrival, none was evident. Clearly he was still buoyed by the optimism I'd noticed earlier in Grassendale.

Calum and I politely refused drinks. Danson remained calm when I told him I'd reached Gordon Merrick in Spain, but light flared in his eyes when I gave him the Chester address. I saw him catch his breath, flick a glance at Becky, and he leaned forward as he sipped his whisky. When I told him how we'd seen Michael and Peter leave in a Volvo driven by a woman wearing dark glasses he dismissed the news with an impatient gesture.

'They're young men, that's normal behaviour. They'll probably be out drinking till dawn and turn in to work with hangovers.'

I shook my head. 'That's not the way I read it. Three days ago I was warned off by a couple of thugs and didn't take the hint. Since then I've spoken to the police, questioned people I believe are or were suspects, found James Cagan's corpse and located the house in North Wales. That led me to Merrick. Tonight I went to his house in Hoylake, then phoned him in Spain. At that point I was getting very close to your boys. It seems somebody decided it was too close.'

'Fine, if that was possible, but they're not clairvoyant,' Danson said, picking out the fault in my reasoning. 'Where'd you phone

Merrick from, your car?' He saw me nod, and spread his hands. 'So there you are. The person who's doing this couldn't possibly know you phoned Merrick.' And then he realized what that meant, and his eyes widened.

'I agree,' I said. 'I don't like coincidence. I ring Gordon Merrick; fifteen minutes later we get to Chester and Frank's boys are doing a flit.'

'Or being taken,' Calum said. 'Kidnapped for the second time. One more step on the way to that nasty reunion we were discussing.'

'No,' Becky said. 'I don't think they've been taken. Gordon Merrick won't have changed, and the Merrick I knew would fight to keep those boys. If they really have gone, then he's behind it. He phoned, told them they had to get out in a hurry and he was sending someone with a car.'

'If that's true,' I said, 'then he's spirited them away from us *and* from the kidnapper who has been playing nasty games.'

'It's the only plausible explanation,' Danson said. 'That, or my suggestion that they've simply gone out.'

'Perhaps. But to accept either of those theories is to underestimate some very dangerous opposition.'

'Come on! What has this clever opposition

done so far? Sent me a few photographs and cryptic cards. Buried a man who died a natural death in hospital. Fired half-a-dozen shots in a dark cemetery and thrown a few punches.'

'Bad enough, surely,' I said. 'The cards and photographs are the reason you came to me.' I hesitated, mentally bracing myself, then said, 'Sadly, Frank, there's now much more than that.'

And, to his terrible distress, I told him about the brutal murder of Claire Sim.

★ ★ ★

The police were talking to Frank Danson in the kitchen.

The jarring ring at the bell had caught Danson with his face in his hands, fingers in his white hair, the room in shocked silence at the bombshell I had dropped. Ginny had been with him for five years, but Claire had been in at the beginning and had grown with Danson Graphics. Though playing a minor role she had helped shape the business. Her loss was hitting him hard.

At Becky's nod I had answered the front door to a detective and a uniformed female officer. Despite his grief Danson had followed me out of the living-room, greeted them with a wan smile and led them through to a back room — probably the kitchen. When I returned to the living-room Calum was already talking to Becky Long. His voice was low, but in it there was the edge of steel designed to cut through nonsense.

' . . . don't go along with this bloody rubbish about an evening out on the piss. Or Merrick sending a friend with a car. Those lads have been snatched. We almost had 'em, now they've gone.'

Becky Long was stubbornly shaking her head, yet I sensed a weakening in her stance. I returned to my seat, considering what Calum had said.

'This is how it went,' I said. 'The woman we saw in the Volvo was the woman behind the original kidnapping. We were getting too close, so she acted. We all agreed there's going to be a meeting between father and sons, so sooner or later she was going to take the boys somewhere, either by coercion or against their will. We forced her to make that second enticement or snatch sooner rather than later.'

Becky still had to be convinced. 'How did you force her?'

'By phoning Merrick.'

'And we're back to square one, the big flaw in your reasoning.' She smiled sweetly.

'Merrick's not involved. We now agree on that.' She raised her eyebrows, admitting to her change of heart, and I nodded acceptance. 'So how *did* the kidnapper know about the phone call?'

'I don't know. Unless you've been talking. Did I tell you we don't entirely trust you?'

She let that one go with a slight frown and pushed her lips in and out, thinking hard. A door opened and the murmur of talk from the kitchen became louder as the police prepared to leave. Absently, Becky reached across for Danson's glass and sipped his drink, savouring the fiery spirit as she allowed herself the ghost of a smile.

'It's very simple, isn't it, Mr Private Investigator. You've got a mole.'

'Not possible,' Calum said. 'Most of the important talk is restricted to three of us — Jack, Sian, me. Stan Jones I would trust with my life. And I believe you know Manny Yates.'

The front door slammed. Frank came into the living-room looking drawn. The police had been unable to add to what I'd told him. No clues. No suspects except a tall man with dark hair who'd been seen at the murdered woman's flat.

'That was you, wasn't it?' he said.

'Yes.'

There was no point in saying I was the probable cause of Claire's death. An investigator investigates. Without poking his nose in, he gets nowhere.

'We were talking about moles,' I said. He looked confused. I explained with a smile. 'Calum scoffed at the idea. I tend to agree.'

'Either way,' Becky said, 'you're going to have to come up with some fresh ideas — and keep them under wraps.'

'The ideas I have are not fresh, but for them to be usable I need some co-operation.' I looked at Frank. 'You came to Calum's asking us to take the initiative.'

'That's right.'

'Well, if this was a second snatch it's left us back where we started. And although I had a promising lead — a red-hot lead: I'm sure Claire had the answer to the James Cagan puzzle — she's now dead and so is Cagan.'

'So what do you want?'

'The answer lies in the past and I think that's the only way we can break through. I can trace Cagan's relatives through the police computer. I'm willing to do that. But I need to do some digging into *your* past, and for that I need some co-operation.'

And now he could see where I was going. His lips tightened. I could see him framing a negative response.

'When I came to your house with Calum,' I said, 'you told us that Jenny was universally loved; that you had no enemies, that *she* had no enemies.'

'True. Every damn word of it.'

'Aye, but that's only as far as you knew at the time,' Calum said gently. 'You see, we've been considering possible motives for the original kidnapping. One was that someone was desperate to have children — and that seems spot on now we've discovered Gordon Merrick. The second, which actually came to mind first, I believe, was that someone wanted to get at you; to cause you pain. The way this wee woman is acting it looks as if we're right again.'

Talk of motives had got Becky, the ex-police officer, sniffing the air. She was looking at Frank, waiting for a reaction. He remained stubbornly silent.

'Frank, what about Carol?' she said.

Pain flickered in his eyes, and his nostrils pinched as he sucked in a deep breath.

'Carol was Jenny's closest friend,' Becky said to me. 'Frank would know if *he* had enemies at that time, but if you want to know about Jenny before she got to know Frank, then it has to be Carol.'

'Frank,' I said softly.

He promised to find the address, and phone number.

We walked out into the misty night with something achieved, one small victory to chalk up.

But as Calum and I drove back to Grassendale I couldn't help recalling that the last young woman I spoke to about Frank Danson had ended up dead.

24

Day Six — Saturday 15 October

Breakfast the next morning was the usual coming together of two ex-army bachelors in Calum's kitchen for a greasy fry-up washed down with hot coffee during which animated fighting talk was like friendly fire ricocheting off walls and ceiling.

As always it worked surprisingly well.

I knew I had to trot down to Admiral Street, talk to Mike Haggard and tell him I was the debonair man with dark hair who'd been seen talking to Claire Sim. In limbo between the finished and despatched 15th Light Dragoons and the Ned Kelly sets I hadn't yet brought in from Wales for painting, Calum was going to meet Georgie for coffee on Allerton Road then wander back to the flat to await my return.

From there we intended to drive to Runcorn and talk to Carol, if we could reach her and she was available. Frank had come through with the phone number and address and told us Carol's maiden name had been Crane, she had married, changed her name to

Vaughan and retained that name when her husband died.

Calum got through to her on his mobile just as I was leaving. I stopped at the door, he mimed 'twelve o'clock' and I gave him the thumbs up and clattered down the stairs.

It was half eight. We had stacks of time.

★ ★ ★

Haggard's lip curled; Willie Vine chuckled; I looked suitably abashed.

'You'll be gobsmacked to know we've been treadin' on your heels, Ill Wind,' Haggard said. 'Where you've been, we've been — sometimes before you knew where you were goin'. We know you talked to *both* girls. We know you went house huntin' in Wales and got a Bangor solicitor to dig out old deeds.'

'That's really very funny,' I said. 'So what else did Becky Long tell you?'

Haggard grinned and dug out a king-sized cigarette.

'I don't think there is any more. You're up a creek without a paddle, a place — '

'I've been many times. Yes, all right.'

Haggard struck a match, filled the air above his desk with swirling coils of smoke and sat back smirking, his jacket swept open to reveal a wrinkled white shirt.

I smiled and let him have his moment, while secretly I was drawing comfort from what he *hadn't* said. They must have spoken to Becky last night after we left and with Frank Danson already in bed. Becky had told them enough to keep them happy, but nothing of importance. They knew what I'd done, and why — hadn't Haggard himself suggested the house in the photograph was located in Wales? — but they didn't know what Sian had unearthed in Bangor, they were unaware of the phone call to Spain or the address in Chester and they had no idea to whom I would be talking at midday.

Which didn't stop Willie Vine from watching me with a shrewd gaze that would spot the smallest of slips — and next I had to beg for more of his expertise.

'You're right. I'm getting desperate,' I said. 'I'm convinced James Cagan played a part in the Danson kidnapping but I can't dig up any evidence. He's dead, so I need to talk to his relatives. The quickest way of locating them — '

'Try Walton cemetery,' Haggard said. 'Right, Willie?'

I groaned. 'All dead?'

Vine nodded. 'Father and mother. He was an only child.'

'Another door closes.'

'When one door closes, another opens,' Haggard said, and grinned toothily around his cigarette. 'Shut it on your way out.'

★ ★ ★

I had climbed into the Quatro and slammed the car door when my mobile rang. It was Becky Long.

'Get round here fast. He's got another photograph. You were right, but that doesn't make it any easier for him.'

It was just after nine and most of the rush-hour traffic was still heading towards the city centre. I sped along almost empty roads and got to Long's house in Woolton in ten minutes. I expected to find Danson a broken man, but Long had either exaggerated his despair or got it completely wrong. He was all fired up.

'Another one came,' he said. 'This one . . . well, see for yourself.'

'Was it delivered to your house, or here?'

'Here. While we were sleeping.'

'So they know exactly where you are, what you're doing.'

He had a jacket on and was pacing, which was difficult for a tall man in Long's small living-room. He seemed unconcerned with

254

the idea that he was being watched, and pointed to the coffee table where another of the now familiar photographs was lying face up. Still breathing hard after running from distant parking place to front door, I picked it up — and within seconds of looking at it I had caught some of his excitement.

It was the usual 5″ × 5″ print taken from a medium format negative. Again it showed two men clad in black, their balaclava helmets off and clutched in their hands. Again they had been posed against a wall. This time it was whitewashed, emulsioned, whatever it is they do to walls — and for an instant, because of their garb, I assumed it was the same two kidnappers. Then memory kicked in. I'd already seen a photograph of the two kidnappers without their black gear. Two fair-haired men. The men in this photograph were also fair-haired, but they were two different men and I didn't need to ask Danson their identity. Just as the two children playing in Gordon Merrick's garden in Wales were clearly the same two boys shown struggling with the kidnappers, so these two were recognizable as those same two boys now grown into men.

'This time there's no doubt,' I said softly, putting the photograph on the table.

Danson nodded. At that moment I don't

think he could speak. Becky Long touched his hand. I saw his throat move as he swallowed.

'Nothing else? No card?'

'Oh yes.' He found his voice. Cleared his throat. I thought I detected moisture in his eyes.

The card was in an envelope. He handed it to me. I took out the card. It said:

See you soon, Daddy

'Nasty.'

'Is it?'

'The message is intentionally cruel. It tells us something about the sender.'

'We agreed that everything has been leading up to a meeting. This proves it.'

'Frank, your boys are in the hands of criminals. The woman who kidnapped your children associates with thugs, vicious killers. They assaulted me and murdered Claire. Yes, we all agreed everything was a build up to an eventual reunion. But we also agreed, you agreed, that the meeting would not be . . . pleasant.'

His laugh was brittle. He stopped his pacing and shoved his hands into his pockets.

'So what would you do? Your kids were snatched, your wife committed suicide, you haven't seen your boys for twenty years. Now you get a message: see you soon, Daddy. And you know, you're *convinced*, that very soon you'll get another message telling you where you'll be able to meet them.' He took a deep breath, let it out, steadied himself. 'Your *sons*, Scott. So tell me — what would you do?'

'I'd go to see them,' I said, 'of course. But I'd be under no illusions, and nor should you be. Your boys are being dangled before you as live bait, Frank. You are being lured to a certain and probably very unpleasant death.'

I'd hoped to shock him. I missed by a mile.

'I'm already dead. The next massive step will bring me back to life.'

'Don't do it. When the message comes, call the police.'

'No.' He shook his head, something like panic in his eyes. 'No, definitely no police. I hired you to find them — '

'Then leave it to me.'

But he wasn't listening. 'When the chance comes, I'll take it. Wherever they are I'll go to them. But until that happens — until I get that last message — I've got a business to run.'

'On Saturday?'

'Do your toy soldiers have weekends off?'

He smiled absently, not really listening to his own words, then turned, kissed Becky on the cheek and walked out. I heard the front door slam, his footsteps receding.

'He's running to keep things moving,' Becky said. 'He wants everything to happen now and believes hanging around here with you is making the clock's hands turn more slowly.'

'You're a philosopher.'

'I could be a snitch. The police came last night.'

'Don't worry about it. I've spoken to them.' I smiled. 'And I like your circumspection.'

'Thank you, kind sir,' she said, and executed a mock curtsy. 'So when do you see Carol?'

'Midday. Which means I must get going.' I hesitated. 'Sooner or later the kidnapper *is* going to deliver those instructions.'

'I know. If I can intercept them I'll hold them without showing them to Frank until you get here. If Frank gets hold of them first I'll keep *him* here for as long as I can.'

'Do you agree with me? This has all been building up, leading up, to a meeting between father and sons, but the meeting has always been a means to an end, the end being to get Frank Danson to a place of isolation and take the . . . revenge . . . to its logical conclusion.'

'Murder him? I've absolutely no doubt. And if they murder Frank, of course they must also murder those two boys.'

'Which means,' I said, 'that by allowing himself to be enticed to that place, Frank Danson is signing his sons' death warrants.'

★ ★ ★

I was back at Grassendale just after ten. The sun had broken through yesterday's cloud cover and was warming the hazy air over the Mersey. When I climbed the stairs, Calum was in the kitchen, and once again I could smell that faint, subtle perfume: I knew Georgie had come back to the flat with him.

I tossed my coat on a chair and went through.

'She gone?'

'Aye, ten minutes ago.'

'How is our new consultant?'

He pulled a face. 'The bastard she calls husband has been at the grog again. She's got a nice wee bruise on her cheek, passes it off as nothing while doing her best to hide it with make-up.'

'Why doesn't she walk out? Surely if she needs somewhere to stay you could put her up here . . . '

I left the thought trailing, waiting for his reaction. None came — which I thought unusual — so I busied myself with the percolator while he sat at the table flicking idly through the *Telegraph*. The coffee pot bubbled its lazy hypnotic tune. I leaned back against the work top as it did its work and the water spurting into the little glass dome gradually changed colour, and I told him about the visit to Haggard and Vine, the latest photograph to drop onto Frank Danson's mat.

'So we now know for certain that when we saw them last night in that Volvo, they were being taken.'

'Aye, but cleverly and without force,' Cal said, folding the paper. 'The woman fed them some cock-and-bull story. The force would come later when they realized they'd been duped.'

'Mm. The trap's been set and baited,' I said. 'Now the woman will get word to Danson in the usual way.'

'And he'll drop everything and go running to see his bairns.'

I nodded. 'I tried to dissuade him. Even suggested he go to the police, but he's having none of it.'

'*You* could go to the police,' Calum said, 'behind his back.'

'I should have given Haggard the full story when I was there — but I didn't.'

'Which means you don't intend to.'

I shrugged, got out the mugs, looked to Calum for his nod and poured two coffees. I sat across the table from him. We drank, mulling over this and that. I looked up. He was watching me with dark, amused eyes.

'Us against them,' Calum said. 'The Lone Ranger and Tonto. The two musketeers.'

'Three. I've got a funny feeling Sian's expertise will come in useful.'

'That would restore the numbers, but she's in Wales.'

'So were Pat Maguire and Bill Fox.'

'Aye, but they were murdered by Calvin Gay who's now out of it and anyway had no links to Danson.'

'He knew James Cagan.'

Calum frowned. 'A lot of people must have known Cagan. And now we've mentioned him, wasn't Gay next on your list of interviewees?'

'Yes, but I've got a hunch I'll learn more about Cagan from Carol Vaughan.'

'A long shot.'

'We're due some luck.'

We pushed back our chairs and carried our coffee through to the living-room. Reflected sunlight flooded in through the window; in the pale-yellow light of autumn the bright streaks of paint on Calum's empty work table lay like scattered shards of a fallen rainbow.

Georgie's scent was much stronger. For some reason it was making me uneasy.

Calum chose the settee and stretched out with ankles crossed. I sat in my leather chair and glanced at my watch. Half ten. We'd have to leave for Runcorn soon after eleven.

After a few more moments of silent meditation, Calum stirred.

'Why,' he said, 'am I looking at a microcassette recorder when neither you nor I own one?'

I followed his gaze. A gold-coloured Olympus Pearlcorder lay on the empty easy chair.

'Where did Georgie sit?'

'There.'

'Then it fell out of her handbag.'

All gangling legs, he unfolded himself, came off the settee and plucked the recorder off the chair. He glanced at it. Turned it over. Flipped his stained wire glasses out of a top pocket and perched them on his nose. Examined the back of the recorder.

'Well, well,' he said in a voice without tone.

He looked up with a flat gaze and tossed the recorder to me.

I looked where he'd been looking. A small piece of white paper bearing a name had been stuck on the back with transparent tape.

The name was Claire Sim.

'Jesus Christ!'

Very carefully, Calum said, 'Why are we surprised? You mentioned the recorder to Claire, she didn't deny owning one.' And he looked at me, and waited.

'And Georgie having Claire's recorder merely suggests that they know each other,' I said. 'But now we're opening a can of wriggling worms, aren't we? It was Georgie who told me I should interview Danson's girls. Why didn't she tell me she knew Claire? And think about this: Claire has a recorder, and *we know she visited James Cagan*. So now the recorder ending up in Georgie's handbag is beginning to look very suspicious.'

'Aye,' Calum said. 'Because what we're now asking ourselves is did Georgie *also* know Cagan?'

I turned the recorder over again, pressed the eject button. The little door popped open. There was an Olympus microcassette inside. Very little tape was on the take-up spool. Just enough to record . . . what?

I slid it out, held it between thumb and finger and waggled it so Calum could see.

'What d'you reckon?'

He put his mug on the table, stayed on his feet, prowled. Stopped at the work table. Slammed his fist down on it with a growled oath. The Anglepoise jumped. The shade at the end of the arm quivered. Calum looked at the edge of his hand. In the reflected sunlight it was multi-hued. With a thin smile he shook his head and picked up a damp rag to scrub at his hand. Suddenly Georgie's subtle perfume was drowned by white spirit.

Calum slipped off his glasses, absently rubbed the lenses with the filthy rag.

'Was Georgie ever here when we mentioned Cagan?'

'Yes. The first time I met her. Haggard and Vine had just left. You and I discussed what had been said.' I thought back. 'Amongst other things, Cagan's name came up.'

'Then if she knows him, she also kept very quiet about that. She was, if I can use a cliché, keeping consistently mum.'

I was running the tip of a finger round the rim of my mug.

'A thought occurs — a very obvious thought.'

'To both of us. Simulfuckin'taneously. Because everything is indeed becoming *blindingly* obvious.'

He dropped the rag, slipped the glasses in his pocket and returned to his coffee. Drank it down, still standing, still restless.

'Put that cassette back in.'

'Mm. We have to play it.'

'Yes, we do. Because if Claire visited Cagan

in the hospital then passed the recorder to Georgie, what I think we'll be listening to is that nasty bit of low-life's last words.'

'Important words. That's why Claire Sim sat with him for the best part of a week.'

'Right. Because until that last day he said bugger all.'

I slipped the cassette into the recorder and snapped the door shut, pressed rewind, waited until the tape hit stop then pressed play.

There was a faint hissing.

I turned the knurled volume knob.

We both recognized the slow, spaced, bleep . . . bleep . . . bleep . . .

'Intensive care,' Calum said.

Then the voice. Tired. Threadlike. Too thin to hold a man's life suspended.

'*Georgie,*' it said. '*Georgie . . . I* know. *I* know *what you did.*'

The voice trailed away. There was nothing but harsh, wet breathing. Agonizingly slow. The pause between breaths became longer. In those pauses, the listener strained with the dying man, willing him to breathe. Then there came the murmur of a woman's voice. Tender. Encouraging.

'Claire,' I said.

Calum held up his hand.

Cagan again. '*I . . . know what you did.*

265

*And I know what you did made her . . . made
Jenny . . .* ' Then more harsh breathing. Then,
stronger, insistent, '*But I don't care, Georgie
. . . because I love you, don' I . . . an' I
always have an' always will . . .* '

The recorder clicked.

I let my pent breath out slowly, touched the
thin film of sweat on my forehead.

Calum sat down as if his legs had given up.

After a long moment I said, 'When you dig
really deep into that can of worms, a bruise
on a young woman's cheek that was a purple
relic of a domestic row becomes a wound
suffered when a serious crime was committed, last night, in Chester.'

'And because we both know she likes
playing nasty games,' Calum said, 'we need to
ask ourselves if that recorder fell out of her
bag, or was it left on the chair deliberately.'

'Doesn't matter.'

'Aye, it does. Because if it was an accident,
we still have time — '

'No. Accident or deliberate, she'll realize by
now that we've got it, we've listened to it, and
she'll have to make a move.'

'Why?' Calum laughed. 'I know her first
name — and that's all I bloody know. She did
it, she kidnapped those kids twenty years ago
and last night she drove them away in
someone's Volvo. But where she is now, where

they are, I have no bloody idea. And if she can lie low for twenty years . . . '

'All right. She knows we've got the recorder and she knows we're on to her. So now we decide what we're going to do and we do it now when she can't possibly hear us and — '

Calum was watching, listening to my every word. But my abrupt stop left him flummoxed. He turned his head, looked comically about him, back at me.

'What?'

'I thought I heard someone outside.'

He looked confused. I lifted a finger to my lips. Nodded towards the door.

'I'm going to look,' I said clearly. 'Someone's messing with the Quatro.'

He followed me out, shut the door and clattered down the stairs after me. When we were outside, the scent of the Mersey in our nostrils, the flat as good as a million miles away, I stopped.

'Last night Becky was right and you were wrong. She asked how anyone could possibly know that we'd phoned Merrick. She'd already given us the only possible answer — a mole — and you'd rubbished the idea. But think about it: the first time Georgie came to the flat she made coffee; she was in the kitchen — on her own. On the way out she stopped at your work table, leaned over it, rested her hands on it in a perfectly natural way. And today we've learned something about her that makes it obvious what she must have been doing.'

'Too bloody right,' Calum said with an expression somewhere between rage and despair. 'A mole doesn't have to be human. That woman's not only been leading me up the bloody garden path by my beard, she's bugged the whole bloody flat.'

25

They were easy to find. Georgie had stuck the second gleaming little button under the edge of Calum's work table when she leaned over to admire the dashing Light Dragoons on her way out. In the kitchen, while making coffee, she'd stuck the first one behind the strip lighting that was screwed under one of the cupboards. Since then all conversations taking place in either room would have been picked up and sent to a receiver. I guessed their range would be short, so a car or van must have been parked in one of the adjoining streets for several days.

Once we knew bugs had been planted it was easy to look back and see where Georgie's mistakes had gone unnoticed. I recalled how, in her second visit, she had stated that looking for the kidnappers' relatives was pointless — when we had never discussed that possibility in front of her. And, of course, there were those times when someone was always one mysterious step ahead of us: the graveyard and the man with the rifle; Sian telephoning from Bangor, Becky searching for Merrick's address — calls received or made in Calum's kitchen.

I was no electronics expert, and neither was Calum. That meant a change of plan. Manny Yates would have the information we needed, or the right contacts. Calum would take a taxi to Lime Street, and consult.

Why? What information did we need? Well, the sudden leap that had taken the valiant PIs struggling with the Danson case from knowing absolutely nothing to knowing a bit more than nothing had spurred my brain into furious activity. It occurred to me that if shiny little buttons could send information to Georgie, they could do the same for us. When Danson jumped into his car and raced off to meet his boys I'd make certain he had one of those shiny listening devices taped to his underwear. What I needed from Manny Yates was a crash course in electronic surveillance equipment. I had to know what kind of receiver we needed, its range, where to site it, how to power it and where to get one.

Of course I'd quickly figured out that because they were Georgie's buttons she already had a receiver, and no matter where I put the bugs we would all be gleefully listening to the same broadcast. The way round that was to squash the irritating little bugs underfoot. That would be done, but it didn't really matter. The only conversation I was interested in was the one between Georgie and Frank Danson when they finally met. Georgie would be listening to that without electronic assistance. I intended to be very close, and definitely within striking distance.

★　★　★

Carol Vaughan, Jenny Danson's closest friend, lived off Mersey Road, which was pretty close to Runcorn Old Quay Lock and the River Mersey. I somehow found my way there from the Silver Jubilee Bridge by taking the Bridgewater Expressway and zigging and zagging the Quatro in a general westerly direction. For all I knew it was the right way, the *only* way to get there, but when I knocked on her door and she let me in I didn't ask because I was too damned dizzy.

Perhaps she noticed. She offered me a cup of tea, I accepted and asked for two sugars. She did my bidding without demur, but in my eyes she was a rake-thin vegetarian marathon runner and somewhere between my knocking on the door and taking the first sip of sugary tea I had gone down in her estimation.

'James Cagan,' I said, balancing cup and saucer. 'Have you heard of him?'

'No.'

'He was a small-time crook who died recently. I'm certain he's linked in some way to Frank Danson.'

'And the kidnapping?'

'Mm. Possibly. I don't know.'

She'd jumped to the right conclusion. I wondered how.

My smile was pensive. Hers was mischievous.

'I do know a little of what's been going on. From Becky. And I'd love to help Frank.'

'That's a relief. That you know, I mean. It saves time.' I sipped some more tea, chose some words. 'Frank told me that he and Jenny had no enemies. He went further: he said Jenny was universally loved. But someone, somewhere, must have hated one of them.'

'To take their children?'

'Possibly that, but not necessarily — '

'Oh, come on. It was a woman, wasn't it? According to what the police dug up at the time. And for a woman to kidnap and murder two little boys was the most wicked — '

'They've been found. They're alive and well,' I said, mentally crossing everything crossable.

'My God!' Her hand went to her mouth.

'We know who took them — more or less.

We know where they were taken to and where they live now. Sadly, we believe that woman has taken them again, with some very nasty help. We all believe — Frank, Becky, and Calum, the man who phoned you — that she is going to bring Frank and his boys together somewhere, and . . . and harm them all.'

'You mean murder them.'

'Yes.'

'Call the police.'

'Frank refuses.'

'Ignore him.'

'He doesn't trust them. I believe we need a more . . . softly-softly approach.'

She proved my assessment of her wrong by searching for a cigarette and lighting up. Or do marathon runners smoke? There's a joke there, I know, but it was the wrong time and place and there was no one to listen so I sat there in silence and waited while Carol Vaughan gathered her thoughts.

'I read about you.'

'So did Frank.'

'It was in the *Echo*. You found someone who'd been dead a long time. The write-up said you're very good.'

'I'm trying to live up to my reputation.'

Small talk. She was buying thinking time. Her smile was distant.

'There *was* something, back then. Ongoing, as they say nowadays. Something Jenny lived with. Something she never, ever, mentioned to Frank.' She blew smoke sideways, flapped it away with a hand. 'She was being stalked.'

'Christ!'

'He was a young man. About her age. He never harmed her — never approached her. But he was there. Two or three times a week, sometimes more often than that. And it went on forever.'

'Forever?'

'Yes. Before she met Frank. Then when she was courting; when she was married; when she had Michael, then Peter. And then . . . then the boys went missing and she killed herself.' Her eyes were misty. 'That's what I would have done. I mean, how could anyone go on . . . ?'

'Why weren't the police told? They were investigating a double kidnapping, for goodness' sake. And you're telling me now there was a mystery man, a stalker . . . '

'Jenny wouldn't hear of it.'

'What — she *liked* having him around?'

'Don't be bloody stupid. She decided he had nothing to do with what happened. The kidnapping. And that was that.'

Carol could tell me no more. I'd ruined her

day so I finished my tea and we exchanged pleasantries and I left wondering if I'd got anything. I now had a mysterious stalker, a young man with an obsession. But Danson's two boys had been kidnapped by a woman and sold to a senior policeman and his wife who could not have children and it became one of those happy-ever-after sagas you find in *Reader's Digest* with the crime bit missing.

Where on earth did James Cagan fit into that?

*   *   *

When I got back to Grassendale Calum was still down town. I reached him on his mobile. He was in the American Bar enjoying one of Manny Yates's everlasting liquid lunches. In the background I thought I could hear Jones the Van's harsh cackle. Good. As a team there was no one to rival those two middle-aged scallies and the raw-boned Highlander I would trust with my life *and* my toy soldiers. Manny was mentor and PI know all with bells on, and it would not have surprised me if Stan Jones of the grey beard and rusty white van had a degree in electronics and in his spare time moon-lighted for MI5.

Calum left me with a cliff-hanger. He'd got some interesting mail. No, he wouldn't say what it was because he had the wee bugs in his pocket and once bitten and all that crap . . .

I could hear Yates and Jones the Van chortling into their drinks as I switched off, and I wondered what nonsense and misdirection they'd been feeding into those hungry, ever-alert little bugs.

Driving along familiar roads is done on automatic pilot, and once out of the Runcorn maze and onto Speke Road I'd been able to think freely. I'd gone to Carol Vaughan hunting for Frank Danson's enemies and left with a stalker. Maybe it was far-fetched to pin that crime on James Cagan, but it would have been foolhardy in the extreme to rule him out. In a few inspired moments I came up with a couple of simple questions that would help to bear out or quash the notion — help, but not make absolutely certain — and the men I knew who would provide the answers spent most of their waking hours in a green-painted office in Admiral Street.

★ ★ ★

Before going in to talk to Haggard and Vine I made use once again of the miniature miracle that is the modern mobile phone. Vine would have loved the alliteration; square-jawed Dick

Tracy would have been sneering in his grave because he wore something similar on his wrist some seventy years ago — but that was in an American comic. I used mine to phone Danson's office. He wasn't there, and I remembered that it was now Saturday afternoon. So I tried his home, caught him and told him what I wanted.

'Frank, I need the date of your marriage.'

'Nineteen-eighty-two. Michael was three in eighty-five, Peter two. That was when they were . . . ' The pause was painful. 'If you need the exact date of the wedding,' he said, 'it was May the first — Jenny's birthday.' He hesitated again. 'Is that enough? Can you tell me why you want to know?'

'Later, Frank, but yes, thanks, that's all I need.'

It was only when I clicked off that I realized neither Calum nor I had thought to tell him how close we were to a breakthrough. For a moment I hesitated, wondering whether to ring back, wondering whether to tell him about Georgie and how he should be on the lookout for a petite, shapely but deadly woman with a voice warm enough to melt ice. Then I dumped the phone in the door pocket and climbed out into the sunlight.

I was parked on double yellow, the computer was in Willie's upstairs office. Risky

277

if clampers were out in force, but what I wanted from the literary DS should not take long. I left the car where it was — reminding myself to ask Manny Yates to acquire for me one of those blue disability cards that I could prop on the dash — and ran across the road.

Mike Haggard had nipped out for what George Bush the younger had famously been photographed calling a bathroom break. Vine was in front of the computer and more than happy to continue playing with his new toy. I sat down by Haggard's desk and explained what I needed.

'James Cagan was a recidivist, so he'll be in there somewhere. I'd like you to look at his record.'

The keys clicked. On the screen the display changed rapidly.

'Nothing juvenile,' Willie said after a few moments. 'No Borstal. He started late, was first arrested for . . . ' — he looked across at me — 'the attempted rape of a young woman in her twenties.'

'When?'

'Eighty-two.'

The year of Danson's marriage.

'And after that?'

'Oh, he was a regular offender. Shoplifting, burglary, theft from cars . . . '

'But nothing big?'

'Not until eighty-six.'

And that was the year after the kidnapping, the year Jenny Danson took her own life in a bath of bloody water.

'What did he do?'

'Attempted murder. Another young woman.'

'Bloody hell!'

'Enough?'

'Mm. More than. Suddenly, all is clear.'

'Tell me.'

'I'm pretty sure that from the very early eighties until eighty-six, Cagan was a stalker.'

'Makes sense. He stalked them, they weren't having any so he snapped and attempted to rape and murder — '

'No.' I cut him off. 'Just the one woman in all that time. Jenny Danson. And he never touched her.'

'You've been working hard.'

'Hard enough to find the kidnapper — although that was probably luck.'

He rocked in his chair, his eyes suddenly guarded as behind them his mind raced. This was a twenty-year-old crime I was talking about. The police had got nowhere. Vine was as genuine as they come, but even he could see the benefits to be gained by nipping in and stealing my thunder.

'Who is she?'

'A woman called Georgie.' I grinned.

'Sorry, that's all we know — and we don't know where she is.'

'Lucky for you it's not buried treasure.'

His chagrin was evident. I was willing to bet he was hoping for Haggard to walk in and play bad cop.

Before that could happen, I stood up and turned towards the door.

But I was too slow.

Haggard banged his way in like a bad-tempered bear, burly, shirt sleeves folded back, loose tie dangling and a cigarette trailing smoke from his big fist. He looked at me, glowered, and went to his desk.

'Ill Wind's cracked the Danson case and found the kidnapper,' Willie Vine said. 'Nearly.'

'So the first three words say it all,' Haggard said, and puffed his chest out as Willie Vine grinned.

'Oh, and we've found the two boys who were kidnapped,' I said. 'Nearly.'

I ducked out and jogged down the corridor listening for the sound of Haggard's heavy glass ashtray crashing against the inside of the door. It never came. He was probably still preening at Vine's appreciation of his lame joke.

26

I caught up with Calum in Manny Yates's office after again using the mobile phone. I was going out of my way — or maybe not, because I wasn't sure what I was doing or *where* I was going next — but I made the trip down town because Calum and the Lime Street PI were talking bugs and I was intrigued by Calum's earlier cliff-hanging exit.

The sun had been shining all day but had now disappeared behind swollen banks of cloud. I listened to the radio as I drove. The forecast was for persistent heavy rain. High tides would cause rivers to back up. Flooding was expected in North Wales and in particular in the Conwy Valley. The news aroused my sympathy for householders in places like Llanrwst and Trefriw, but left me reasonably smug: Bryn Aur did not flood.

When I reached Lime Street the rain had already started.

'Surveillance-capable technology's what you're after,' Manny said, when I had shaken my wet jacket all over his floor and settled in a chair.

'What's that, modern jargon for big ears?'

'Yeah, and it's not exactly kids' stuff. Unless you want something simple, like stickin' your ear to a glass tumbler held against the wall separatin' you from the suspect. That won't sound too clever on your PI's report, though, so what you tell your client is you used an acoustic listening device.'

'I'd need a long glass. I'm guessing we'll be something like a quarter of a mile away from Danson and the kidnapper. The conversation will probably be inside a building of some kind.'

'Bionic ears are OK, but not over that distance; they look like a dinky Sky satellite dish connected to head-phones and you point it at the subject. Ultrasonic'll work well over a much longer distance. You can also get optical or laser devices that pick up voices because they make glass windows vibrate.' He grinned. 'Trouble is, so does passin' traffic and a high wind — and those devices are expensive.'

I looked at Calum. 'Who's he trying to impress?'

'Listen an' learn,' Manny said, sitting back expansively. 'Once an understudy, always an understudy. If you're following a car, maybe a bird dog or bumper beeper's what you want. You use a magnet to stick them underneath the car — ' He broke off, fired up a Schimmelpennick cigar and puffed smoke with a frown while he thought. Then he said, 'Nah, too much trouble to set up, for the 180° version you need two aerials, four if you're using a 360° model, so . . . '

'Postpone the crash course, just tell me what's wrong with something like these?'

I pointed to the two shiny buttons Calum had placed on the edge of the desk. They'd been expertly disabled: someone had flattened them with a hammer.

'Nothing,' Manny said. 'They're radio frequency thingies, your classic bug. That's what you want, only better. The really good ones can be switched off by remote to save the batteries.'

'Come on, Manny, it's a conversation we'll be listening to not a five-day Test match.'

'Aye, but that's when Danson gets wherever he's being taken,' Calum said. 'It could be anywhere and take an inordinate amount of time if the malefactors transporting him resort to evasion or diversionary tactics.'

He was straight-faced as he spoke, but a devil danced in his dark eyes.

I looked at Manny and said, 'See what you've started with your hi-tech mumbo-jumbo? If it goes on like this we'll need three dictionaries just to say hello.'

But Manny was already up out of his chair. He walked over to the window with his mobile, a chubby little man in tight waistcoat and baggy pants, and began talking on his cordless phone.

I turned to Calum. 'So what did you get in the mail?'

'Proof. Something we badly need. Georgie planted those bugs, and the recorder told us she knew Claire Sim and James Cagan — but so what? We were left making assumptions; nothing we had was evidence that she was guilty of kidnapping.'

He'd been fumbling inside his leather jacket and now he tossed me an envelope. Inside there was a folded piece of blue notepaper and a photograph.

The photograph showed a woman walking away from a parked car. She was carrying a child. There was a very indistinct figure some way behind her, also carrying a child. That figure, and the background, were blurred. Distance was fore-shortened, and I knew the photographer had used a long zoom lens. The photographs were probably taken without the subjects' knowledge.

The woman in the foreground was young. Some twenty years younger than when I last saw her in Calum's flat.

I unfolded the note. The message was written in blue fountain pen on textured Conqueror paper.

I took no chances. When the boys were delivered to me I wanted a record of the person I was dealing with. This is that record. The woman was known to me as Georgie. I assume she was the woman who was involved in the kidnap of Frank Danson's boys.

There was a scrawled but recognizable signature.

Gordon Merrick.

★ ★ ★

When Manny Yates came off the phone he had the address of an electronics wizard who kept all sorts of surveillance equipment in his garden shed and sold it to people involved in industrial espionage. We drove straight there — it was out Knotty Ash way — and when we left the street of back-to-back terraced houses after some hard bargaining we were carrying a powerful receiver, heavy batteries to power it, and a brown envelope containing a couple of bugs. The garden shed had been in a back yard. And what we really had, according to Manny, was surveillance-capable technology, to wit, sophisticated radio frequency listening devices.

From Knotty Ash we drove straight to

Grassendale. When we got there Frank Danson's car was parked against the kerb and he was walking up and down on the grassy bank, his white hair glistening in the rain. The weather was getting colder and wetter, but there was such an intense, burning light in his eyes from the unquenchable fire within it was a wonder steam wasn't issuing from his ears.

He'd had a visit from Georgie, he said. We were all set.

★ ★ ★

Three o'clock in the afternoon and we were in a huddle listening to Frank Danson's startling and unexpected news while minds galloped ahead thinking tactics and strategy.

The kitchen was the ideal place for it. Liquid lunches make Calum drowsy, and in there the chairs are hard and close to an unlimited supply of hot, strong coffee. The black moggy lying purring in its basket with heavy-lidded yellow eyes — perhaps musing on its sexuality — had the relaxing effect on the body of an hour's yoga while leaving the brain alert, and in the centre of the table the radio receiver and two shiny bugs kept those alert brains suitably focused.

'I can't believe how *nice* she was,' Danson said.

'A poison message delivered in honeyed tones by a wee, deceitful bitch,' Calum said.

I looked at him. He shrugged, but was unabashed.

'She's clever and she's got nerve,' I said.

'No. She's got my boys,' Danson said, 'and that makes her untouchable.'

'So what's the plan?'

'Well, she knows you're on to her — leaving that recorder was a slip, by the way, but that wasn't what forced her to act. It had already done its job. She heard you announce Merrick's name, heard Becky come up with his address; when Becky and I had left Calum's she heard Calum saying it was time you were off to the seaside. She knew you were going to Hoylake, knew where that would lead you, and practically broke the sound barrier beating you to Chester.'

He smiled sympathetically at our disquiet; knowing your conversations have been recorded doesn't lessen the shock of having them thrown back in your face.

'A bitter pill to swallow,' I said. 'Or a couple of them,' and I nodded at the bugs. 'OK, so that's how it happened, now what's she going to do?'

'She's driving a Ford Ka — but you know that,' he said, this time smiling apologetically at Calum. 'I'm to expect her at dusk. She'll take me to the boys. She won't tell me where, or how far — I don't know *anything*. And if there's any sign of pursuit, I'll *never* know; I'll have blown my one chance of ever seeing them again.'

The drum of torrential rain was a monotonous, incessant accompaniment to Danson's words. I listened to him, I took it all in, but all I could register was disbelief. Twenty years of torment and, one way or another, it would come to an end when a man and a woman drove away in a red car built for Noddy and Big Ears. And that brought a smile to my face, because when Danson was whisked away into the dark and the rain we would indeed have very big ears.

I put a hand out, touched one of the bugs with the tip of a finger.

'These are not capable of tracking the car. What they do is send sounds and voices back to this receiver. So when you're sitting alongside Georgie speeding off to Christ knows where, I want you to be very crafty.'

'Needs must, and all that.' He nodded. 'I've read all the detective novels. If she asks if I'm wearing a wire, I'll let her search me. When she's reassured I'll stay quiet for a while then start making off-hand remarks, cunningly slipping our location and direction into the conversation.'

'Almost certainly one-sided,' Calum said. 'If she's got this far on her wits she's not going to give much away.'

'She won't need to. I'm not likely to be lost, wherever she takes me, and I can babble away with the best of them.'

'Well, we've wrapped up one case in a disused windmill, another in a luxury yacht, faced a taxidermist who'd lost his marbles and a woman who'd lost all hope.' Calum grinned happily at me. 'I wonder what young Georgie's got up her sleeve? Are we off to a bat-infested cave, an unmanned lighthouse lashed by the raging winds . . . ?'

'Whatever it is,' I said, listening to the rain, 'odds are we're all going to get pretty damp.'

There was not a lot more to say. We could plan till the cows came home but in the end it all boiled down to 'follow that Ka'. The only way out of the close where Danson's house was located was back onto Childwall Priory Road, and I intended to be parked there when Georgie's little red Noddy car came zipping onto the main road. Complications were limited to guessing which way she would turn; if I guessed wrong, well, the road was wide enough for a U-turn, and if we lost them we had Frank whispering cunningly into the bug. It would be tucked away somewhere intimate. The precise location we had left to his ingenuity.

It was four o'clock. Frank Danson would get home by 4.30, squirrel away his bug and sit twiddling his thumbs. The heavy cloud cover meant dusk would fall early. I estimated Georgie would pick him up some time between 6.30 and 7.00. I wanted to be in position on Childwall Priory Road by 6.15.

We tied up loose ends and toasted our anticipated success with hot laced coffee. The room was humming with nervous tension. Danson picked up both gleaming bugs and slipped them into his pocket. At the last minute I'd decided he should take a spare. Belt and braces; better safe than sorry.

As he walked out and clattered down the stairs I quickly found my mobile and phoned Sian.

'Hi, Jack.'

Two syllables, and my knees went weak.

'It did the trick, Soldier Blue.'

'My hot news from Bangor?'

'Mm. We located Merrick in Spain, had a chat that gave us the boys' address. But we were foiled. The kidnapper had planted bugs in Calum's flat and knew exactly what we were doing.'

'That's a first — and Calum must feel

great. But what about this kidnapper. Do you know his name?'

'Just the one. And it's not a he. It's Georgie.'

There was a silence in which I could almost see the shock in her blue eyes.

'My God, yes, of course,' she said at last. 'I'm so relaxed down here it had slipped my mind that we were looking for a woman. But Georgie of all people! And poor Calum. First the bugs, now this, a real double whammy.'

'Information is so sparse you know almost as much as we do and you're out there in deepest North Wales where mobile signals are, to be polite, notoriously fickle. Which, to get to the point, is why I phoned.'

And then I told her what I wanted her to do.

27

If you saw Cary Grant in *To Catch a Thief* then you'll know how we were dressed. Wearing black from head to foot, soft shoes for soundlessly creeping up on villains and swashbuckling, devil-may-care attitudes, we were cat burglars preparing to prowl. But this was Britain not the French Riviera. The weather was deteriorating into a Hong Kong-style typhoon so we carried with us vital accessories that would allow cat burglars who might eventually look like drowned rats to function adequately.

Calum had a tiny, horn-handled skean-dhu poked into his sock, I had a Swiss Army Knife with a dinky pair of tweezers and, in the Quatro's boot, I made sure there were two pairs of Wellingtons and a green-and-white golf umbrella. We were armed and dangerous, no matter what confronted us we would be well-groomed, dry of foot and, brandishing the umbrella, nonchalant as hell.

You could also say we were deluded, and daft as brushes. But not daft enough, on a stormy night, to leave behind waterproofs that were wrapped tightly around heavy rubber torches on the floor under the glove compartment.

We were sitting in the Quatro facing towards the Five Ways as the rain swept in sheets across the sodium lighting in Childwall Priory Road. Calum was in the back seat alongside the heavy receiver, headphones up in his ragged grey hair. Rich chuckles at the idea of two grown men poncing about in black gear under a huge golf umbrella like down-market John Steeds led to a natter about Haggard and Vine's frustration, and considerable speculation over where the two young men were being held. But it was all for a purpose, casual waffling intended to calm nerves that were jangling like fire irons. I'd been deliberately sanguine when we drank our toast with Frank Danson, but nothing had happened before or since to alter my conviction that the kidnapper had been playing a deadly game that would end in the death of Danson and his two sons.

'She's a woman, attractive, and a delight to be with,' Calum said, once more reading my thoughts, 'but Georgie's past record makes for a gloomy prognosis. We should have talked him out of it.'

'Waste of time trying. He put the question to me: if they were my sons and I was faced with the same situation, what would I do? I gave him the only possible answer.'

There was a moment of quiet.

'Worrying about Frank has reached the stage when we have to worry about what we're likely to face when we get . . . wherever,' I said, flicking on the ignition and using the wipers to clear rain from the windscreen. 'We've joked about it, but if Georgie's alone when she collects Frank then the two lads are being guarded by a man, and that man's a killer.'

'I'm no longer sure she needs male help. She's dainty, smells intoxicatingly sweet and has a cute smile, but any woman with a Heckler and Koch VP70 has, what, eighteen little helpers all lined up ready to spit in the eye of the opposition. Meaning you and me.'

'Could be a Beretta 93R. That would give her fifteen.'

'Or maybe she's got the equivalent of your wee penknife,' Calum said, grinning. 'A Swiss Sig Sauer Pistole with its puny nine rounds.'

'I reckon a Glock because it's seventeen per cent plastic and much lighter — '

He stopped me with a raised hand and a murmured word of caution.

Fifty yards away a little red car was emerging from a side road. It turned left, away from us. There were two people inside. The driver was a woman; in the passenger seat, a tall man with white hair: Frank Danson.

'Must've been at Danson's house when we parked,' I said, 'because we certainly didn't see it go in.'

'Oh yes, it was.'

The car — or Ka — accelerated away from us, heading for Childwall Five Ways and Queens Drive.

'Look away, you silly bugger,' I said softly, as Danson turned his head to look back as I started up and set off in pursuit.

'Luckily for us,' Calum said, 'those bugs are uni-directional.'

'If that means they only work one way and she can't hear me — I know.' Then I realized what he'd said. 'What d'you mean, oh yes, it was? Are you telling me you're switched on?'

'In both senses. But the receiver's been switched on for a while now. Bit pointless setting off without doing a dry run, the bloody things could be duds. And listening to Danson has taken my mind off your inane prattle.'

'Bastard!'

He chuckled. 'He had a coffee while he was waiting. Or tea. Dishes were rattling. Then there was a ring at the bell.'

'You heard him talking to Georgie.'

'Of course.'

'And said nothing!'

He didn't answer. I heard movement and glanced in the mirror to see him settling the padded headphones over his ears. He was squinting past me, his eyes on the road ahead.

'Right now, that rain helps the chasing pack,' he said.

The Ka's rear window was reasonably clear but there was a plume of dirty spray being kicked up. Traffic was light. Drivers were leaving long gaps between vehicles and, with a clear view ahead, I was able to hang back. Georgie would find it very difficult to spot a tail.

The little red car swooped down to the Five Ways, indicated and turned left into Queens Drive. We followed at a distance and watched it shoot straight through the green light at Woolton Road then down the slope and turn sharp left at the roundabout into Menlove Avenue. I was already anticipating her moves. I'd been reasonably confident that I knew where she would go ever since the notion struck me and I phoned Sian.

She reached the lights at Hunt's Cross Shopping Park and turned left again, and I nodded sagely.

'Runcorn and the M56,' I said. 'That's where she's going.'

'Then full speed ahead to Welsh Wales?' He

caught my nod. 'Well, I suppose it did start there with a double murder — it was wet then, and tonight there'll be a soggy welcome in the hillsides.'

'A very *warm* welcome, for us; maybe too hot for comfort. I just hope she's heading for high ground.'

After that we drove in silence, Calum concentrating on the earphones as we hissed along roads that were like shallow rivers and took us through Hunts Cross and Halewood and onto the fast dual carriageway that was Speke Road.

I was once again driving on automatic pilot, sure in my own mind of the direction Georgie would take if not her final destination. The former was confirmed before we reached the motorway when Frank Danson began talking idly to no one in particular in a way that would feed us information.

'Heading for the A55,' Calum said. 'The road noise is bad, I think Frank must have put the bloody bug in his shoe, but he's rambling on, watching the world go by and telling her he used to take the boys to the coast when they were bairns.'

'So the A55 — then where?'

'No word yet.'

I'd anticipated an even easier ride when we hit the M56, cruising along with the Ka a bright red dot always in sight, but it didn't work out that way. I'd forgotten about the darkness that closed down when Runcorn and the lights of the Weston Point Expressway were behind us. Once on the motorway the red Ka became a pair of tail-lights lost in a host of similar lights, dancing, glowing pinpoints blurred by spray. With Calum cosy in the back seat, padded earphones like warm earmuffs and eyes closed, I lost myself in some kind of reverie in which Sian figured strongly, and so lost our quarry.

'Bugger.'

A grunt. 'Put your foot down.'

'I'm doing seventy. There's a police car on our tail.'

'We've lost her.'

'I know that.'

'No, I don't think you do.'

I glanced in the mirror. 'What's happened?'

'Georgie saw through Danson's coded messages. They got into an argument. She told him to hand over the bug or she'd stop the car and kick him into a ditch. He gave it to her, she said something like 'Bye-bye Calum' and the last I heard was a load of popping and spitting and crackling. I think she chucked both bugs out of the window.'

The police car was so close to my boot we could have been connected by a rigid tow-bar. As I stared impotently ahead into driving rain and clouds of spray that, lit by the red glare of speeding tail-lights, was like thin smoke hanging over a burning city, I could almost hear the sound of a Ka's engine howling away into the night.

For my liking, the sound I was imagining was too much like a clever woman's shriek of triumphant, devilish laughter.

It was time for Plan B.

28

'Where are you?'

'Exactly as planned: I've reached the lay-by on the A55 about half-a-mile before the long run downhill at Rhuallt.'

'Great, because we've lost them. Danson was wearing the bug, and it was going well. But his chattering must have alerted Georgie. She caught on and gave him an ultimatum, and that was the end of surveillance.'

'But she's coming this way?'

'Oh yes. We're passing Stanlow refinery now. She's some way ahead, so I'd say she'll be with you in under half an hour.'

'What am I looking for?'

'A red Ford Ka, going like the wind. Georgie driving, a white-haired man in the passenger seat. If your eyes are sharp, you'll recognize Danson.'

'Right. I'll be onto them like a leech.'

'And keep us posted.'

'Any thoughts on where they're going?'

'My hunches are getting so accurate I'm scared stiff. Let's just see what happens.'

We closed on that note, as cryptic as spies, as cool as close relatives.

I flipped the mobile to Calum. He connected the hands-free and stowed the phone in its holder. With the radio receiver listening to nothing but the roar of passing traffic transmitted by a radio frequency listening device lying in a pool on the hard shoulder — and rapidly fading away in our wake — he'd switched off, wriggled his tall frame over the squab and joined me in the front.

He looked at the phone, made sure it was still switched on.

'I'm impressed with your planning, but your communication with the hired help stinks.'

'Mm. Sorry about that, but a hunch is only a hunch — '

'And a good cigar is a smoke?'

'Right.' A match flared. The warm car was filled with the familiar aroma of Schimmelpennick tobacco. 'I left you in the dark, but called on Sian and her trusty Shogun. If I was wrong, no harm done. But it seems I'm at least part right, and that Japanese tank of hers will come in handy if rivers burst their banks.' I flashed a sideways grin. 'Plan B's working because we're a well-oiled team. But losing that bug means we've got to get much closer at journey's end. Like, in the same room as at least one murderer.'

Two trucks were blocking the inside and middle lanes as one tried to overtake but lacked the power. I pulled out, screamed past and stayed in the outside lane.

The police car had peeled off at the M53 turnoff to Birkenhead and I was free to motor. Taking the M53 in the other direction at that junction was the quickest, all-motorway route to the A55. I guessed Georgie would have gone that way. But it was several miles longer. I calculated that at night it would be just as fast to follow the M56 to its end, swoop down through Queensferry and join the A55 at Ewloe.

I kept the speedometer needle on 90 for most of the way, slowing only for the two roundabouts above Queensferry, catching the one set of lights on green and ignoring the 50mph limit where the motorway passed through the town. We made such excellent time that when we raced up the long hill and onto the A55 I was looking in all directions for the red Ka, half expecting to catch it in the mirror as it raced up behind us.

Fat chance.

The mobile rang. It was Sian.

'The Ka's gone through and I'm on its tail,' she said, her voice a disembodied whisper over the racket of our engines. I could hear talking in the background and guessed she had the radio on. She was ex-army, an expert in survival techniques. With bad weather closing in all the time she would keep all lines of communication open, listen constantly to the latest news and weather updates.

'There's one problem,' she said.

'Go on.'

'There's a woman in the passenger seat, a man with white hair sitting in the back — and the driver's male.'

I looked at Calum. 'Wrong car?'

One hand plucked absently at his beard as he considered.

'Sian,' he said, 'how close are you?'

'Two hundred yards.'

'Move up until you can read the number plate. It should be an S reg. Last three letters C-U-S or G-U-S.'

The noise of the Shogun coming through the mobile phone rose to a roar as she put her foot down. Ten seconds passed. Twenty. Then she cut back to a cruise.

'OK. S reg, and it's C-U-S so it looks like the right car — but if it is, where did the driver spring from?'

'I don't know,' I said.

'Another thing. They seem to be hesitant.'

'In what way?'

'Slowing, then speeding up — then dropping to a crawl. I think they're listening to the weather report on Radio Wales.'

'Bad?'

'It gives us a pointer to where they might be going. The only floods being mentioned are in the Conwy Valley; the road's already blocked at Trefriw. If they're heading in that direction they're bound to be worried. Out there they've got hostages, bait, whatever you care to call those boys. They'll be locked in, possibly in danger of drowning.'

'Where are you now?'

'Marble church at Bodelwyddan.'

'I think we're closing the gap. From now on we'll leave the phones open.'

'If we're heading into the hills we could have trouble with the signal,' Calum said.

'By then,' I said, 'we'll have a good idea where they're going.'

★　★　★

We didn't catch up with Sian.

We passed the ghostly white needle of the marble church's spire fifteen minutes after Sian had taken the Shogun through on the Ka's tail. As we left the lighted section of motorway at Bodelwyddan, Sian was following the red car across the Conwy bridge with the floodlit castle towering above her and the rain and salt spray driving in off the harbour.

The last time we'd been there it had been a calm night and I'd been sculled across the still water to a luxury yacht where unknown dangers lurked. Tonight looked like being a replay but with different combatants and a different field of battle; I knew in my heart that, once across the bridge, Georgie would head inland.

Then Sian started talking.

'She's taking the B5106, up the west side of the river. If she's hoping to get past Trefriw, she's out of luck.'

'We'll be in Conwy in ten minutes.'

'OK, but I'm leaving the coast *now*, and this is where the mobile's signal gets iffy.'

'Doesn't matter. If she motors on past Ty'n-y-Groes she'll be boxed in.'

'Right, but once you start up the valley keep your eyes skinned. If she stops I'll try to get the Shogun deep into the trees, then watch and wait at the side of the road and wave you down. Look out for my bright blue GOR-TEX waterproof and straggly blonde hair.'

I chuckled. 'A damsel in distress. If there's any traffic, you'll stop the lot.'

She didn't come back. When I looked at the mobile it was doing a network search. We'd lost touch for the foreseeable.

'My guess is those lads are being held in a

caravan,' Calum said as we pushed on towards Colwyn Bay.

'Why?'

'I'm remembering a recent conversation. Georgie saying how her old man loved fishing, how he had this caravan where he'd go weekends. Remote, she said. Close to the river.'

'And you've just remembered?'

'Opportune moment, wouldn't you say?'

'Bit bloody late. Did she say where?'

'Remote. Close to the river.'

'You're repeating yourself.'

'*Ad nauseam* if you persist, because it's all I know.'

Ten minutes passed, and I was skimming across Conwy bridge. The castle loomed. I swung left under its towering walls. Within minutes we'd left the residential area behind and were in dark, open country. The wind had strengthened. Trees were tossing wildly overhead and shedding yellow leaves that skittered dizzily across the slick road. Every time we hit an exposed stretch the buffeting wind rocked the car and threatened to slew it sideways as I hung onto the wheel. From time to time we drove through hollows where water had cascaded down from saturated fields and the flood slowed us to a crawl that left a muddy bow wave creaming in our wake.

There was no sign of life in Tal-y-Bont. Dolgarrog was a ghost town where dim lights on tall concrete poles peeked at us through shifting curtains of rain. And, thinking ahead, I knew we were running out of road.

A couple of hundred yards from Trefriw Wells Roman Spa the headlights picked up a patch of blue topped by a glint of gold. I pulled into a muddy lay-by from which a steep track snaked into the woods.

The door opened. Sian climbed into the back seat with a rustle of wet GOR-TEX.

'There,' she said, and pointed across the road.

In the reflected light from the headlights I could see the wooden gate leading to a field bordering the river. It was half open. Feet had churned up the mud, but failed to hide the ruts dug deep by a car that had driven in with wheels spinning. On the very edge of the light I could just make out the red of Georgie's Ka. Foolishly, she had started across the field and made no more than thirty yards before getting bogged down.

Already the creeping flood waters were lapping and gurgling at the half-buried tyres.

The car was empty.

29

We donned Wellington boots and waterproofs and pulled the hoods over our heads. Calum grabbed a torch and splashed across the road and into the field.

'I cruised up without lights and stopped a hundred yards down the road,' Sian said. 'I could see them churning up the ground trying to get the car into the field. When they got bogged down they were splashing about, falling over in the mud and screaming at each other. Then the man kicked the car and they all struggled across the field in that direction.' She pointed. 'Danson went willingly. But he would do, wouldn't he?'

'Calum reckons there's a caravan.'

'There's something over there. The light's weird, have you noticed; dark, yet strangely luminous. If it is a caravan, it's perilously close to the river.'

'Georgie's dad used to go fishing.' I watched Calum slipping and sliding back towards the gate. 'How long ago did they start walking across the field?'

'Wading, you mean. Ten minutes, no more

than that. I brought the Shogun up, put it in the woods.'

Calum was back with us, breathless, grinning like a schoolboy.

'Aye, the caravan's there,' he said. 'There's lights and everything, it's like a bloody beacon reaching out to drowning fishermen.'

We'd moved back to stand under the trees, preferring cold droplets and fine spray to the relentless downpour.

'Inside that caravan,' I said, 'there are now three prisoners being held by Georgie and an unknown killer. There'll be some talk; it might drag on, or it might be over very quickly. If we don't do something, eventually we'll hear three shots.'

'So we go over there and one of us knocks on the door and goes in when invited,' Calum said. 'The other sneaks around to see if there's another way in.'

'That's two, Cal,' Sian said. 'I count three of us.'

'Aye, but this is man stuff. Girls wait here with the oranges.'

'Jack?'

'He's right.'

Her blue eyes flashed in the dark. She turned her head and looked up the track into the woods. Then she nodded.

'All right.'

'All right?'

'Yes.' Her smile was sweet. 'I acquiesce, so what are you waiting for?'

'Inspiration,' I said. 'Calum's plan stinks.'

'You've got four hundred yards and maybe four minutes to think of a useful alternative,' Calum said, and started across the road.

I pulled Sian to me and gave her a cold, wet kiss.

'Something to remember me by,' I said, 'if I don't return.'

'Bugger off.'

So I did.

★   ★   ★

Lights glowed yellow in the windows of hill farms on the far side of the valley, beacons warning us away from a watery grave. The rain swept across the field, driving into our faces, plastering waterproofs to bodies. The flood waters were streaming in from the swollen river, snaking down gullies and turning the field's hollows into lakes that shone like flat mirrors in the eerie light. That left us some high ground soaked only by the rain. Along that slippery, serpentine route we squelched our way towards the caravan.

'Easy to get cut off,' Calum said.

'We can both swim. Away from the river

there's no current. Flood waters form still, silent pools.'

'Bloody big ones.'

Close up the caravan was revealed as a weather-worn aluminium shape from which all paint had been stripped by years of sun, wind and rain. Over it an enormous oak loomed, black and heavy of bough. I shone the torch low. The van stood on rusty wheels with two flat tyres. Iron stands at the four corners had seized up or rusted away. It looked like a lopsided lay-by café without the tatty pennants. I got the urge to giggle; if I opened the door, maybe they'd all fall out and spill their tea.

Net curtains covered the windows. I guessed they were using a gas lamp. In its light, shadows moved across the curtains.

'So,' I said.

Calum grinned. Rain was streaming from his beard. His dark eyes were alight.

'You or me?'

'I look tame. If I stroll in like a rambler taking a wrong turning it'll lull them into a false sense of security.'

'Aye, and just then the hard man pounces and saves the day.' He nodded. 'Off you go.'

I sensed him drift away into the rain-swept night. I sucked in a deep breath, gripped the heavy torch tightly and took a couple of soggy steps up to the door. Reached out a cold, wet fist and hammered on it.

Then I walked in.

* * *

My immediate impression was of warmth and mildew, stale sweat, the soft hissing of the gas lamp that was as painfully bright as burning phosphorous.

The smell of fear in a sudden silence.

And Danny Maguire, lean and dark, swinging around with his mouth wide with shock.

'Evening all,' I said, and closed the door.

The interior of the van had been stripped to form one bare room. At the far end the two young men I'd seen in the final photograph were sitting on the floor. Their backs were against the wall. In the crumpled black outfits they were dirty and tired. Their bound wrists rested in their laps clutching crumpled balls of wool I knew must be the sinister balaclavas. In the bright light their faces were a stark white. Their breathing was too shallow, their eyes a little too wide and never still.

Frank Danson was sitting on the floor with his back against the long wall. Wrists bound, white hair plastered to his skull, pants stiff and slimy with mud. One of his shoes had gone and his sock was half off but he couldn't have cared less. He had eyes only for the two boys.

Georgie, dark-haired, a mud-spattered delight, was sitting on an old oil drum.

She was holding what looked like a Walther PPK.

It was pointed steadily at my chest.

★　★　★

'Jimmy looked after me,' she said softly. 'Jimmy Cagan.' She was taking up where she'd left off, talking to them, not me — although it was me she was controlling with the deadly little pistol.

'When I was a kid. When I'd been beaten by my dad. He'd dry my tears, then use his dirty hanky to wipe away the blood. We grew up together, me depending on him. So when he got hurt . . . '

'He didn't get hurt,' I said. 'He was a stalker, harassing Jenny Danson.'

'Jenny?' Danson's head shot round.

'Jenny *Long*,' Georgie said, and her eyes were angry. 'Oh, he got hurt all right. When she married *him*.' She jerked the pistol at Danson. 'Jimmy was hurt so bad he went . . . wrong . . . and so I made *him* pay.'

'But you fucked up,' I said, deliberately coarse, goading her; reducing what was happening to something between just the two of us; shifting her mind from Danson and his two sons.

'I . . . ' She shook her head, her face white in the harsh glare, eyes suddenly bleak with torment.

'Jenny couldn't take what you'd done. She killed herself. You took those two boys and sold them to Gordon Merrick, but by doing so you took away the woman Cagan was obsessed with.'

'Loved. He *loved* her.'

'But you took her. *You* — and he went off the rails.'

'He forgave me.' I watched the rise and fall of her breasts as she fought for control; saw her knuckle white on the pistol's trigger. 'He forgave me. He loved her, he always had. But at the end it was *me* he loved, you *heard* him — '

'But you weren't *there*, at the end. You sent Claire, the wife of one of your criminal friends, because you knew if you were seen with him it could ruin your plans.' I saw her squeeze her eyes shut. 'And when he went off the rails all those years ago, it was *your* fault, but you did nothing. You could have taken your revenge then. Wiped Danson off the face of the earth. For Cagan. Instead, you waited twenty years.'

'I waited for Jimmy to die.'

'Why?'

'Because when the soft bugger wasn't in clink he was stalking Danson,' Danny Maguire said. 'Danson was his last link with the bloody woman. She knew if she killed Danson she'd as good as kill that bloody pervert.'

Through all the talk he'd been standing back against the wall. Now, with that sudden outburst, the balance of power had shifted. Georgie held the gun. Georgie was the kidnapper. But it was suddenly clear that Maguire was the danger.

'It wasn't Gay who killed Pat and Bill Fox was it — it was you?'

'He was knocking her off. She was my wife.'

'More than that. She was about to go to the police and wrap up a twenty-year-old murder.'

'Her stupid fault.' He jerked his head at Georgie. 'Again. She goes through life creating monumental fuck ups. She was playing with Danson, a cat with a fucking mouse. So why bring Pat in with yet another of those bloody cards?'

'I was warning her off,' Georgie said. Her

voice was strained. There was a sheen of sweat on her pale face.

'*Tipping* her off,' Maguire said. 'Taking unnecessary risks.'

'How did you frame Gay?'

'Georgie got him to play with the gun.' He grinned at me. 'She worked for him part time; she was in the back room when you were talking to him.'

In the sudden silence, the caravan lurched. I thought it was Calum using muscle to bring some life to the party. But suddenly the sound of rushing water was much louder. I looked at Danson. He nodded, understanding what was happening. I saw him look down in chagrin at his bound wrists then, with a swift glance at Georgie, work his legs underneath him. He did it with a grimace, as if bothered by cramp.

Maguire had also felt the caravan lurch, then rock lazily. He moved away from the wall, keeping one hand flat against it to steady himself.

'Enough talk. Time to go, so get it over with. You two, put those balaclavas on — '

'Georgie,' I cut in, 'this is not like you.'

Her smile was bitter-sweet. 'You don't know me.'

'Calum does — and he's not easily fooled. Twenty years ago you kidnapped for revenge.

You're not a killer: Maguire's the killer.'

Maguire laughed. 'She brought them here, together, so they'd die together.'

'No. Maybe that was her plan, but if it came to the crunch — '

'She's right, you don't know her at all. She'd kill, just like she kidnapped for revenge and *gain*, just like she trafficks kids for gain. Has done ever since I provided the baby-sitter, then found out what she was really up to and how it was a fucking big money spinner. For her it was a one off. Sweet revenge and a few thousand quid. For me it was the start — and whether she's liked it or not her feminine charms have been making it work for all those years — '

He didn't finish.

The next lurch was a big one. It was as if a tidal wave had come sweeping down the river to wash across the field. The caravan tilted sharply. Danson's sons yelled in panic as they slid across the floor and slammed against the long wall. Danson was caught with his legs under him. He toppled forward then rolled and braced himself with spread legs. Georgie came stumbling sideways off the oil drum. The shiny pistol flapped dangerously. Maguire was flung away from the wall. They collided in a tangle of limbs, clutching each other, fighting for balance.

Then with a tremendous crash and a splintering of wood and metal, Calum Wick came crashing feet-first through the roof. He hit the floor in a shower of water. The wind moaned across the gaping hole. The gas lamp swung wildly, cracked against the wall and went out.

Eerie light seeped through the hole in the roof. In the dimness I leaped at Georgie and Maguire. I swung the heavy torch with two hands, putting a lot of muscle into the blows. The downward swing smashed into Georgie's face. I heard teeth crack, saw the black stain of blood as she was knocked flat on her back. The Walther PPK slid across the wet floor. Danson scooped it up with his bound hands. I let my body snap back, like a tight spring unwinding. The two-handed backhand swing slammed the torch into Maguire's temple. The skin split. In the gloom his eyes rolled white and he went down in a limp heap.

Suddenly, inside the caravan, there was a sense of intermittent weightlessness, as if we were in a lift that couldn't decide whether to go up or down.

'We're afloat,' Calum yelled.

I leaped for the door, banged it open. It was caught by the wind. A hinge snapped. The waters were swirling across the field. The caravan was moving sluggishly. It was afloat and being carried towards a bend in the river. Once there it would be caught by the current —

'Here, Jack!'

A yellow canoe shot out of the darkness. Behind it a red canoe bobbed and twisted at the end of a rope.

'Cal, get those fellers out here!'

I dropped to my knees, held onto the door frame and grabbed for the yellow canoe. Sian was driving it in with strong sweeps of the paddle. The bows slammed against the caravan. I felt the healing gunshot wound in my arm rip again as my hands closed over the slippery fibreglass, clamped, held. I dropped onto my side, bent at the waist and used the pressure of my thighs against the inside of the caravan's wall to hold the canoe against the doorway.

The flood water was taking the caravan.

'Calum, get those — '

'Here.'

A knee slammed into my shoulder.

'Careful, watch it — '

One of the young men half stepped, half toppled into the canoe. The second followed, landing heavily. The canoe dipped. Water washed over the gunwale.

'Jack, let go, let go.'

Sian dug the paddle deep, ripping the

yellow canoe with its human cargo out of my grasp. She paddled hard, bumping along the caravan. On the end of the rope the red canoe followed, drew level with the doorway. Gasping, I stretched, reached for it. My knees slipped away from the wall. Fingers touching the red canoe, I began to fall out of the caravan.

Then a strong hand grabbed my belt. I was heaved back onto the wet, slippery floor. Calum held me there by sitting on the back of my thighs. I held the canoe tight against the caravan. Frank Danson stepped gingerly into the doorway, steadying himself awkwardly with his shoulder against the frame. His wrists were bound. One hand held the glittering pistol.

Then the caravan hit an underwater ridge. The front end grounded in soft earth. The sudden jerk threw Danson out of the doorway. He went straight over the canoe. I saw the pistol fly into the air. He hit the water flat and went under, came up gasping and hooked an arm over the canoe.

'Not too deep,' he cried. 'Get in, both of you. I'm OK like this.'

Calum eased his weight off my legs and I slid face down into the canoe. I felt it dip as Calum followed. He landed on top of me. A knee cracked the bump on the back of my head. His bony shoulder bore down on my bloody arm. With the weight of three men gone, the caravan lifted, floated. It was much closer to the bend in the river; much closer to the racing current. As we struggled to our knees and watched, it began to move faster, responding to the tug of the river.

Then Sian took control.

'Get that idiot into the canoe,' she yelled, 'then paddle for your life.'

Who were we to disobey?

We got Danson aboard without capsizing. Found the paddles. Began paddling.

And after that I suppose you could say it was all plain sailing.

★ ★ ★

I got through to Alun Morgan on the mobile when we had driven back down the B5106 and crossed the river by the bridge at Tal-y-Cafn.

'If you want to arrest the killer of Bill Fox and Pat Maguire,' I said, 'you'll find him in a caravan floating down the river Conwy. If it doesn't go aground at the wide bend near Bodnant Garden, you should catch it at Glan Conwy or Deganwy. If that fails, alert the Irish coastguard.'

'What do we do with Calvin Gay?'

'Let him go. He was framed. Oh, and if you'd like to be in Mike Haggard's good books, get in touch with him and tell him where to find the woman who kidnapped Frank Danson's kids twenty years ago.'

'Go on,' Morgan said wearily. 'In the same bloody caravan, I suppose.'

'There's clever,' I said, and switched off.

30

'I've never bashed a woman in the face. And I hit her too hard. I heard her front teeth go, saw the blood . . . '

Calum was unsympathetic.

'She was holding a Walther. If she'd shot those three men you'd have been next. You saved at least four lives, three of them worthwhile.' He grinned. 'And don't forget, one of those worthy characters is a client who's going to reward you handsomely.'

'Even so it's enough to make any honourable PI hand in his badge.'

'You always say that,' Sian said, 'and you know what happens.'

Calum chuckled. 'Aye, the telephone rings and the fuckin' ill wind starts blowing . . . '

'Cal!' Sian, amused, looked suitably shocked. Then her expression softened.

'She was a people trafficker, Jack,' she said. 'One of the worst kind: she sold babies, young kids.'

It was breakfast at Bryn Aur, the seventh and closing day of the Danson case which

323

just happened to fall on a Sunday. A day for reflection. Three of those with much to look back on were asleep upstairs. Danson and two exhausted young men who, as Michael and Peter, had been innocents caught in the clutches of a death that was twenty years in the waiting. Which, in the end, came to naught and left them . . . where?

The old bump on my head still ached dully. I shrugged away the confusion of thoughts and reached across for the pot to top up three mugs, feeling the tug of the fresh bandage on my arm. The gurgle of the coffee echoed the noise of the water hissing and streaming across the slate yard. The rain had slackened not a jot and was still dancing on the stones. The oak tree between house and workshop was bowed under the weight of wet yellow leaves that refused to fall. As I glanced out of the window I was taken back ten hours and in my imagination saw bearded Calum Wick with a rubber torch between his teeth, clawing his way up another black oak to wriggle along a heavy bough over-hanging a tatty caravan while listening in dread for the sharp crack of a pistol.

I sighed.

'I suppose, in the end, most of it turned out to be straightforward.'

'Always does,' Calum said, 'with hindsight.'

'Cagan stalked Jenny. When she married Danson, Cagan was distraught. Georgie took her revenge by kidnapping the two boys. But that was too much for Jenny. A year later she killed herself, and so ruined Cagan's life. But now Georgie's hands were tied: she couldn't murder Danson, because Cagan was using him as a link to the dead woman. So she waited twenty years. Then Cagan died in a hospital bed, and the waiting was over.'

'Photographs and cards, with letters of blood,' Calum said. 'And while she was playing sinister games with Danson, she took time out to place the dead Jimmy Cagan where he'd always wanted to be in life but never had the guts to achieve: lying alongside the woman who had been his obsession.'

'You didn't tell us where and when Maguire came in,' Sian said.

'Yesterday he must have been in Georgie's car all the time, lying on the back seat. Twenty years ago, well, he knew Georgie and at her request he provided a baby-sitter — Pat, his future wife. But when the kidnapping became big news he realized what a terrible crime Georgie had committed. From that day to this, she was in his power.'

'He moved in and forced her to make people trafficking a paying game?'

'Mm. The feminine touch. Sweet talking

poverty-stricken single mothers into giving up babies for a pittance, selling them on at five hundred percent mark-up.'

'Jesus Christ,' Calum said, 'you make them sound like chubby plastic dolls from Hong Kong.'

'Maybe that's the way Maguire looked at them. Remember he told me he had kids? I know now he has none. It was just another story.'

'Aye, like Georgie's marriage, maybe.'

'A gold ring and sob story to create sympathy when she was getting to know you.'

Sian pulled a face and carried the empty coffee pot over to the sink. She stood for a minute looking out of the window. Soldier Blue, my blonde, intrepid warrior who had allowed me to venture into battle with a cold kiss of farewell because she knew that when I was out of my depth and in over my head she could come paddling to the rescue. Captain of cavalry in a yellow canoe, with a red one to pick up the sodden infantry.

'What'll happen to Merrick and his wife?' She swung to face us, feminine concern homing in on family issues. 'I mean, what can they have them for? Receiving stolen goods?'

'Neatly put, but I really don't know. Something in the law books will have the answer.' I pulled a face. 'And I don't know what possible arrangement Danson can come to with his boys.'

'Young businessmen,' Calum said. 'So it's for them to decide. They're already living away from home. My guess is things will stay pretty much the same, but with them gradually and willingly getting to know the stranger who's come into their lives.'

'And that's it,' I said. 'Alun Morgan sprang into action. Georgie and Maguire were picked up when the caravan ran aground. Maguire's with the North Wales police and Georgie's in Liverpool. End of story, with everything in the right place though not necessarily in the right order.'

I stood up, yawned, looked out at the rain and thought of toy soldiers and the Ned Kelly bushranger sets I'd been working on when Danny Maguire came a-calling. Calum was here. The workshop was there. I could walk down the slope in the rain and bring everything together to get some work done.

And then, of course, the phone rang.

We do hope that you have enjoyed reading this large print book.

Did you know that all of our titles are available for purchase?

We publish a wide range of high quality large print books including:
Romances, Mysteries, Classics
General Fiction
Non Fiction and Westerns

Special interest titles available in large print are:
The Little Oxford Dictionary
Music Book
Song Book
Hymn Book
Service Book

Also available from us courtesy of Oxford University Press:
Young Readers' Dictionary
(large print edition)
Young Readers' Thesaurus
(large print edition)

For further information or a free brochure, please contact us at:
Ulverscroft Large Print Books Ltd.,
The Green, Bradgate Road, Anstey,
Leicester, LE7 7FU, England.
Tel: (00 44) **0116 236 4325**
Fax: (00 44) **0116 234 0205**